INTO THIN AIR

A DETECTIVE INSPECTOR TAYLOR CASE-FILE

PHILLIP JORDAN

FIVE FOUR PUBLISHING

Jude,

Hope you enjoy this
trip to Belfast.

Continued Success with your
blog.

Best wishes,

P. Jnr

Get Exclusive Material

GET EXCLUSIVE NEWS AND UPDATES FROM THE AUTHOR

Thank-you for choosing to read this book.

Sign-up for more details about my life growing up on the same streets that Detective Inspector Taylor treads and get an exclusive e-book containing an in-depth interview and a selection of True Crime stories about the flawed but fabulous city that inspired me to write, *all for free.*

Details can be found at the end of **INTO THIN AIR.**

Chapter 1

"Aido, it's me. Where are you? Ring me back when you get this."

Aoife Quinn stabbed the call-end icon in frustration and gunned the Porsche Cayenne across traffic, the manoeuvre earning a blaring toot of ire and rapid flash of headlights from a beat-up box van driver forced to jab his brakes to avoid a collision.

"When's Daddy coming home?"

"Daddy's at work, Sophie. He'll be back later," said Aoife.

"Why do you keep ringing him if he's at work?"

Aoife adjusted the rear-view mirror and looked at her daughter in the back seat. Sophie batted a plush toy giraffe off the passenger headrest while her twin brothers, at last, dozed quietly.

The SUV juddered as she hit a traffic calming ramp at speed, the twins' eyes snapping open with the jolt. Their mouths and plaintive wails filled the cabin of the car a second later.

Aoife's phone trilled.

"Aido…"

"No, it's me…"

"I told you I'd sort it. Stop torturing me," she snapped.

The twin cries rose to a crescendo as she pulled up outside

her house, searching in the central console for the gate release fob. She shushed the crying babies to no avail, as the voice over the hands-free continued to speak, persistently talking over Aoife's attempts to interject. She sighed, impatiently tapping the steering wheel as the gates swung open.

"Look, I'm running late. I've just got in and his car's not here. He told me he would speak to you today himself," she said, pulling up outside a double garage, the electronic handbrake whining as it engaged.

"What do you mean you haven't seen him?" She paused as the caller answered.

Aoife pulled the phone from its holder and got out, thumping the door closed and dampening the sound of the cries inside. External carriage lights illuminated as she paced away from the car, the handset to her ear and tossing her hair out of her eyes as the wind kicked up across the dark expanse of manicured lawn, mature cedars and yew trees creaking as they swayed in the strong breeze.

The house was in darkness and she felt a tight knot of anxiety creep into her tummy as the Porsche's internal light bloomed on and Sophie shouldered the rear passenger door open and climbed out.

Aoife turned as a car passed the closing gates, the twins' cries were growing more agitated from the rear seat. She shifted the phone to her other ear.

"Look, I'll have to call you back."

Chapter 2

"How the other half live, eh?"

Detective Sergeant Robert 'Doc' Macpherson ratcheted up the Volvo's handbrake before the car had quite stopped, kicking up a spray of pink pebbles in the process and drawing the attention of a uniformed constable stood at the entrance porch.

"Is she never away back to her school yet?" he said, clicking back the seat and swinging his legs out.

"Here, take your sweets and try not to antagonise anybody else today, okay?" Detective Inspector Veronica Taylor rustled half a dozen brandy balls from a packet and shoved them into her sergeant's huge hand, the paw at odds with the rest of his stature which had earned him the moniker of one of Snow White's famous friends.

"Sure, I just told him the truth…"

"But how many times have I to tell you? If you can't say anything nice, say nothing at all." Taylor pushed her car door closed as Macpherson popped one of the boiled sweets in his mouth and surveyed the lush lawn.

"Whatever happened to free speech?"

"Come on, will you." Taylor moved off, crunching across the pebbled driveway towards the police constable as

Macpherson continued to admire the landscaped grounds.

"Do you think they have one of those ride-on lawnmowers for that?"

"Hi, Leigh-Anne," said Taylor in greeting.

"Ma'am. Sarge." WPC Leigh-Anne Arnold nodded in reply as Macpherson trundled across the driveway towards them. Arnold's hands were shoved into the front of her body armour, and her neck warmer, which she had tucked in tight, warded off the early morning chill.

"Have they still not clocked your birth certificate?" said Macpherson, offering out a brandy ball. "Here, one of these will put hairs on your chest." He hawed out a breathy steam, the plume scented with the heat of the boiled candy.

"My mummy told me never to take sweets off strange men," said Arnold, a twinkle of blue eyes set in a baby face.

Before he could reply, the WPC's TETRA radio warbled on her lapel. She lowered her mouth and responded.

"Sierra-Seven, received. They're here now."

Arnold jerked her chin towards the front door. Taylor nodded.

"Any developments?"

Arnold shook her head.

"None. Mrs Quinn is inside."

"She on her own?" said Macpherson.

Arnold nodded.

"And she still hasn't heard from her husband?" said Taylor.

"He went for a run yesterday morning before work. She found out later in the day he hadn't made it to the office, and when he didn't return her calls or come home last night, she called it in."

Taylor looked out across the immaculate gardens her eyes eventually settling on the mud splashed Porsche Cayenne parked askew in front of the garage doors. A steady stream of school run and commuter traffic thrummed on the road outside the gates.

"Lead the way, Leigh-Anne. Let's see if we can find a simple explanation of where Mr Quinn has disappeared to."

Chapter 3

"Mrs Quinn? I'm Detective Inspector Taylor. I hoped I could ask a few questions about your husband."

Taylor offered a sympathetic smile as she entered the kitchen. Aoife Quinn was rifling through a stack of letters and junk mail, sifting, it seemed, every other page onto a growing pile to one side. In between scanning the sheets, she flicked through a Filofax.

"Mrs Quinn?"

"Sorry." Aoife looked up, her eyes red rimmed through lack of sleep and her voice on the edge of tears. "I'm sorry, I'm just trying to find something. Anything. A note, an appointment I forgot about…"

A phone trilled. Aoife snatched up the untethered landline handset, glanced at the display, and stabbed the end button.

"Bloody nuisance numbers…"

"It's okay. Come and have a seat. This is Detective Sergeant Macpherson. We're here to see if we can help." Taylor laid a hand on Aoife's elbow and steered her away from her fruitless task to a barstool at the wide, marble-topped island.

The Quinn house was a large, detached property on the fringes of Stranmillis. The affluent Malone Road threaded a short distance to the west, while beyond the kitchen's floor-to-ceiling bi-fold doors, the River Lagan meandered toward

Belfast Lough under the shade of tall pines. On the other side of the water lay the lush grassland and swaying wildflowers of the Lagan Meadows Nature Reserve.

"You've your hands full there I'm sure," said Macpherson, moving to stand by the large Aga range. He nodded at a sideboard full of photographs. Aoife Quinn followed his gaze, and the dam of tears broke.

"I'm sorry. I didn't mean to…" Macpherson raised his palms as the woman buried her face in hers.

"Stick the kettle on," said Taylor, pulling a wad of kitchen roll from a holder beside the microwave oven. "It's okay, Mrs Quinn, cases like this usually resolve themselves. Come on, why don't we sit over there and you can tell me what's been happening?"

Aoife choked back a sob with a nod and rose, pointing over Macpherson's shoulder.

"There's coffee brewed. Cups are under there," she said with a sniff.

Macpherson clapped his hands. "I don't suppose you've any biscuits to go with it?"

Taylor's lips drew into a tight line, and Aoife Quinn gave a small, exhausted chuckle.

"Top right cupboard," she said, leading the way to a plush cream sofa and glass coffee table arranged to enjoy the view of the river and wild meadows at the bottom of the garden.

"I'm sorry. State of me." Aoife dabbed the tissue to her eyes and dragged in a ragged breath.

"Don't be. It's just stress. Where are the children?" said Taylor.

"My mummy's. She came over and took them for me last night. Sophie was upset, and I was climbing the walls."

"Sophie, your wee girl? She's the spit of you," said Macpherson, handing her a mug of coffee. "I didn't know how you took it so…"

Taylor watched as the woman wrapped her hands around the mug, seeking its comforting warmth. Her gaze drifted out across the lawn as Taylor's took in the surroundings.

The sitting area was well appointed, the sofa complemented by free-standing chrome lamps and contemporary chalk-painted sideboards, the shelves of which, along with the walls adjacent, held snapshots of treasured family memories.

Predominantly the photographs featured the children; the blonde Sophie in days before the arrival of the twins, in parks, on beaches and posing with her proud parents beside a swimming pool, a certificate and ribbon clutched in her hand. Dotted between those were pictures of her two little brothers, their squashed faces captured in the rictus of joy or placid peace as they journeyed from identical Babygros through a range of matching outfits, balanced on the knees of parents and sibling. Their hair was much darker than their sister's, and they very much had the look of their father.

Sophie Quinn was the picture of her mother. She had the same heart-shaped face and long blonde tresses although she did have her father's eyes. Pictures of Aoife and Adrian Quinn's wedding, holidays, and social events showed a handsome, happy couple, and that contentment seemed to deepen in those photographs of them with their children.

Macpherson clunked a plate of Fortnum and Mason shortbread and a sleeve of Godiva Chocolatier biscuits on the table, taking a seat to Taylor's left and raising his mug in gratitude.

"When did you last see your husband?" said Taylor. Quinn nursed her cup, yet to take a sip.

"Yesterday." She glanced at the clock. "About this time yesterday. He was heading out for a run before he went to the office. I was fixing the kids their breakfast."

"You weren't here when he came back?"

"He wouldn't normally come back. He'd head straight on to work and shower and change there."

"This is routine then?" said Taylor

"Yes. He goes running most mornings. Says it chases the cobwebs away and sets him up for the day. "

"Fair play to him. If it wasn't for my bladder chasing me out of bed, I'd struggle to get up," said Macpherson, whipping a second chocolate biscuit off the plate.

"You reported he didn't make it to work yesterday, though?"

The warble of a mobile phone cut off Aoife's answer. She plucked the phone from her pocket and once again ended the call, placing the phone atop an iPad that lay on the sofa. She shrugged an apology and Taylor gave a half shake of the head to dismiss the need.

Aoife then took a sip of her coffee, quickly following with a second longer gulp and another shrug.

"I didn't know until late. Sophie was in a state by the time I found out. Adrian always takes her to swimming because by that time of the day I'm putting the boys down. She missed it last night." Aoife put her coffee down beside the biscuits. "I'd been trying to reach him and when I realised the time and he still didn't answer, I called Jackie."

"Jackie?"

"Jackie Mahood. He's Adrian's business partner. I thought they had got caught up in something. Adrian is pushing for an expansion of the firm's business and they've had the odd late one with investors."

"What is it your husband does for a living?"

"He's in renewable technologies."

As she said it, Taylor noted the touchscreen panels that had replaced switches and then the integrated sensors that were dotted about discreetly to control light and heat as needed rather than the conventional technologies that could be found in most homes. The iPad that lay on the sofa beside Quinn was no doubt another device that controlled further aspects of her smart home. She considered it for a moment.

"So it was Mr Mahood who confirmed he hadn't made it in?"

Aoife nodded.

"Was that out of the ordinary?"

Aoife shrugged.

"If it was, Jackie never said. They were supposed to have a meeting yesterday, but Jackie said he never showed up."

"What about work? You said he was in the middle of an expansion. Was he stressed with it? Any problems he talked to you about?"

"Not really. I don't think Jackie and he saw eye to eye on some of the specifics but they both understood it would raise the company to the next level."

"Could you give us the address? I'd like to ask Mr Mahood if he has any inkling as to why your husband might skip their meeting."

"I'm his wife. I think I'd have more of a notion if something was going on with Aido than Jackie Mahood." Her tone grew sharp and a scowl crept across her fine features. Taylor offered a sympathetic smile; the woman looked ragged.

"It's just routine, Mrs Quinn. You'd be surprised at what we can sometimes find with just a different perspective. If this expansion deal did have an element of stress or caused worry, Mr Quinn may have kept it quiet so as not to burden you," said Macpherson.

Aoife nodded, her hand brushing the iPad for non-existent crumbs.

"Has anything like this ever happened before?" said Taylor.

"No," said Aoife.

"And aside from work, nothing else you are aware of that might explain the absence?"

"None."

"You've checked his diary, emails?" Taylor pointed at the iPad. "Can you track his phone location from that?"

"It wasn't set up and I've checked his diary and personal mails. Maybe there was something on his work calendars but I can't access those."

Taylor nodded.

"Okay, I know it doesn't feel like it, but, it hasn't been too long and there's probably a reasonable explanation. We'll make some enquiries and arrange an appointment with Mr Mahood. If your husband does get in touch or you think of anything, any small detail at all, let me know." Taylor pulled a contact card from inside her jacket and laid it on the coffee table.

Aoife picked it up, running a fingertip across Taylor's printed name.

"It's just not like him. He's dependable. He's our rock." Her tears bloomed again, and she sobbed, her throat constricted with emotion as she spoke. "Oh God, what if something terrible has happened? What am I supposed to tell the kids?"

Chapter 4

"That's a sin."

DC Chris Walker stooped to closer inspect the deep gouge in the paintwork of the gunmetal grey BMW i8 Coupe. The scar cut a path from the driver's door handle to the rear quarter panel and couldn't be argued away as an accident.

"I wouldn't leave a shopping trolley around here, never mind a hundred grand motor. If you want my opinion, he was asking for it," said Detective Constable Erin Reilly, who stood at the front end, taking a snapshot of the registration and then a wider angle shot of the vehicle in situ with her mobile phone. The car sat alone in a chevroned bay of the Drumkeen Forest Park car park.

Above and around the two police officers, bird song trilled and the keening of wind rustled through mature woodland. The dense canopy and thickets of the forest park insulated them from the rumble of traffic on the main A55 ring road less than five hundred metres away and offered a sense of peace and calm serenity, albeit the park was caught in the noose of the main arterial road, a commercial shopping park and a nearby housing estate.

"He's lucky the wee buggers over there haven't stripped it for parts or raked it to within an inch of its life," added Reilly, offering a nod to the wall of greenery on the other side of which stood the Drumkeen Housing Estate.

Walker stood back to admire the car's unblemished side, tucking in his shirt tail which perpetually worked its way loose, and calming his hair with the palm of his hand, the wind assaulting a long sandy fringe that was deftly cut but failing to hide a rapidly receding hairline.

"Still, it'll cost a fortune to fix that," he said, wincing.

Reilly walked a circuit of the car, examining the vehicle for any other signs of vandalism or disturbance, but finding none.

"We'll need to find him first to tell him the bad news," she said.

She stooped by the rear driver's side tyre where a handful of cigarette butts were crushed on the tarmac, and a sliver of wrapping and a squashed packet lay half buried eighteen inches into a pocket of long grass.

"Hello?"

Reilly stood, catching sight of a woman walking briskly across the car park. Behind her, the facade of the RSPB's (Royal Society for the Protection of Birds) northern headquarters blended into the undergrowth. The old stone walls were gripped in the thick arms of climbers and wrapped in broad vines of Irish and Boston ivy. The building, which had been repurposed by the wildlife charity, was formerly the stables of the Hill family estate.

"Hello, can I help you?" The woman was in her thirties. Dark shoulder-length hair swept around her head as she walked, and she brushed it out of her face, plucking a strand from recently applied pale pink lipstick. She stopped as she reached them, pushing her hands into the pockets of her gilet. Underneath she wore a thick Aran sweater, prepared for both the unpredictable weather and the muddy paths that wound through the woods, with her black jeans tucked into wellington boots.

"Detective Constable Reilly. This is DC Walker. We had a report about an abandoned car?"

"That was me," said the woman. She half turned, leaning toward the old stables that suddenly looked ominous as clouds rolled across the sun, plunging the path to the entrance door and the forest tracks into twilight. "You'll want to come away in, it looks like it's about to bucket." The woman beckoned, then turned on her heels and walked away.

Reilly glanced across to Walker who was looking to the sky as the first fat droplets of rain hit the BMW's windscreen.

Chapter 5

Macpherson's words of goodbye caught in his throat as the gates to the Quinn home eased open on hydraulic rams and a dark green Land Rover Discovery gunned across the threshold, churning up pebbles as it traversed the short distance to pull in behind the detectives' car.

"Is this the fella?" he said.

The Discovery's door swung open violently, cracking against its hinges, and a stocky figure stepped out.

"Not him," said Taylor as the man stamped across the drive. She held up her phone. "Erin and Chris have found the car though."

Macpherson gave a harrumph of approval and eased to intercept the scowling figure.

"Can I help you, sir?"

"I wouldn't bloody think so. Is she in?" As he angled to step around the detective sergeant, Macpherson snapped out a hand, the shovel-sized palm stopping the man in his tracks.

Taylor stepped up and reached inside her coat for her warrant card.

"DI Taylor. Have you business with Mrs Quinn?"

"Too damn right I do? Where is she, and more importantly where's that reprobate of a husband?"

The man was half a head taller than Taylor. What hair he

did have was ginger and shaved to a fine fuzz. The sideburns and beard were much longer and failing to hide the reddening of his cheeks. A tuft of similar hair sprouted from the open collar of a plain white shirt worn beneath a charcoal pinstripe suit.

"Jackie?"

Aoife Quinn stood on the porch, her expression strained as she rubbed the knuckles of one hand with the palm of the other.

"Where is he?"

"I don't…"

"Mr Mahood is it?" said Taylor.

Jackie Mahood jerked the lapels of his suit jacket and cocked his head.

"It is, aye. So have you lifted him or what?"

Aoife Quinn had taken the steps from her porch and was approaching, while Leigh-Anne Arnold had cracked open the door of the liveried police Škoda and was climbing out.

"Let's just all calm down here, shall we? Mr Mahood, we haven't lifted anyone. Mr Quinn is missing and—"

"Done a bunk more like," said Mahood, cutting over Taylor with a scowl and running a hand across his scalp.

"Have you any insights into where Mr Quinn might have gone or why?" continued Taylor patiently.

Mahood opened his mouth to speak, but Aoife got in first.

"He didn't come home, Jackie. He's not here. I don't know where he is." Her voice was husky with emotion.

"Do you think I do?" he snapped.

"Well do you, sir?" said Macpherson. "Because Mr Quinn's diary says he was meeting with you yesterday and this lady only has your word to say he never showed up!"

"Are you serious?" Mahood looked down at Macpherson's gruff expression.

"If there's anything you can help us with, Mr Mahood, it

would be appreciated," said Taylor.

Mahood threw his hands in the air and did a one eighty. When he spun back, he was pointing a finger.

"If I knew where he was I'd carry the bloody head off him," snarled Mahood. He peered over Taylor's shoulder, addressing Aoife. "The investors pulled out last night. Aido shafted the expansion deal because he couldn't keep his trap shut. You want to know where he is? Well, I'll hazard a guess he must be pissed up somewhere working out how to tell you he's just ruined the best chance he was ever going to have of making himself a millionaire, and over what?" Mahood made to say more but cut himself off with an angry shake of his head. "If he shows up tell him to call me."

"Mr Mahood, if you have a minute…" said Taylor.

Jackie Mahood hauled open the Discovery's door in a fit of temper.

"I've not the time or inclination. Phone my PA and she'll set something up. I've a business and a reputation to try to save right now."

Before any more could be said, Mahood slammed the door closed and gunned the engine, the big Land Rover kicking up another storm of pebbles as it roared off down the drive.

Chapter 6

The overgrown branches and thickets of luxurious ivy leaf had been clipped back around the red double entrance door of the RSPB visitors centre to afford access, and Reilly, followed by Walker, entered a short hallway of stone tile floor and whitewashed walls. The hallway ended in another door, wedged open to reveal the room beyond, where, fussing with paperwork at an antique desk was the woman from the car park.

"Just as well I spotted you or you'd have been drowned. I'm Laura Roberts." She beckoned them towards her with a wave and a warm smile, moving away from the desk to flip an antiquated Bakelite switch on the wall, the action illuminating the space and the wall to wall displays of natural wonders and curiosities.

The rain hammered off two plate glass skylights and streamed down the four windows that stretched along the gable wall facing the car park.

"Are these all real?" said Walker, an air of wonder in his tone.

"Yes. Well, they were at one stage. Wonderful aren't they?"

Walker nodded his head, jaw slack as he traversed the aisles, slowly moving between cases of taxidermy and woodland scenes set on raised and roped off platforms.

Dotted between the displays were photographs of the forest, tall information boards and a plethora of drawings and paintings by visiting school children.

Reilly paused beside a small thicket, depicting a red fox pawing the corpse of a fat moorhen. The animal's muzzle was bloody from the kill, its ears pricked back and tail set in rigid alertness, as beady yellow eyes studied the intruder.

Reilly was absorbed by it, her eyes drinking in the details, the matted down of the bird, the raised red fur along the fox's neck and her paw prints in the soft earth.

A series of short staccato barks sent her heart into her mouth.

"Jesus…"

Chris Walker backed up into a tall display of leaflets and postcards, the carousel racing away on its five wheels to collide with a case of roosting songbirds.

"Olly! No." Laura Roberts clicked her fingers as a small Jack Russell terrier continued to grumble, half in, half out of his bed underneath a display cabinet of red and grey squirrels.

"Flip. My heart's doing a dinger here," gasped Walker.

"Sorry, shush you," cooed Roberts to the dog. "Here. Good boy, into bed." She tossed a baked dog biscuit in beside the terrier and he hopped back into his basket, albeit with a rumble of discontent at having been disturbed. Roberts smiled reassuringly at the two startled detectives.

"His bark's worse than his bite."

"We've a sergeant a bit the same," said Reilly, returning the grin. Her eyes drifted back to the fox which watched her warily. "So, the car, Mrs Roberts?"

"Please, call me Laura."

"You said it's been abandoned?" continued Reilly.

"It's been there since yesterday morning. Hasn't moved an inch. Please." Roberts indicated the two seats parked opposite her own on the other side of the desk.

As Reilly sat, she pulled across a pamphlet resting on the edge of Roberts' desk, the cover showing a murmuration of starlings in flight against the sunset backdrop of the Queen Elizabeth Bridge.

"Stunning isn't it?" said Roberts.

"It sure is. You can see this from our canteen window in Musgrave Street. Is this true?" said Reilly, holding up the leaflet. Its stark title proclaimed the gregarious songbirds' numbers were in free fall, the rapid rate of decline enough to prompt action by environmental and protection groups in a bid to stave off potential extinction.

"Tragically, yes. We are estimating a fifty per cent dip in flock numbers over just the last few years which is astonishing. I've never seen anything like it, and although our research is in the early stages and we are looking at the climate change impact on food supply, there is almost certainly a chain of causation linked to the scale of building development and redeployment of our land use." Laura Roberts sighed. "You'll have seen it for yourself driving over, the city limits have stretched far beyond where they were when we were children."

"Makes you glad for pockets like this," said Walker.

"Islands of tranquillity amid the madness, definitely." Roberts smiled again, the corners of her eyes wrinkling. Her skin was tan from a life spent outdoors, and a band of freckles running from cheek to cheek gave her a youthful look. Walker blushed under the glare of her grin.

"Who's responsible for seeing to the gate, Laura?" said Reilly. Roberts puffed out her cheeks.

"Could be me or one of the groundsmen. I opened up yesterday and today. That's when I noticed the car was still here," she said.

"And it's unusual for vehicles to be left overnight?" said

Walker.

"We try to dissuade it." Roberts nodded to a small polite warning notice by the entrance door. "We're close to the estate and while the gates stop cars and motorbikes, you can't stop the kids from climbing over and getting up to mischief."

"But it's still an occasional occurrence?"

"Yes."

Reilly looked at the woman, her face puzzled.

"So why report this one?"

"Well, that's the thing. I've seen the owner of the car several times over the last few months. He arrives and heads out the red track on a run, he's usually back within the hour and then leaves."

"Do you know him?"

Roberts pulled a face, eyes narrowed and mouth twisted noncommittally.

"I know him to see, and you can't exactly miss the car."

"No, she's a beauty," said Walker with an appreciative nod which Roberts returned.

"Spoke to him?" said Reilly, pencil poised above notebook, confident that Roberts would get to her point, eventually. She gave the same expression.

"Hello. Nice day." She shrugged and raised her eyebrows. "I was in here yesterday morning getting sorted for a meeting when I heard a car speed in. You just knew they were flying by the revs, then skidding to a stop. I went out to set the record straight with the driver and there was a jeep, just abandoned, you know? Behind the car, blocking it in." She motioned in the general direction of the BMW.

"Okay," said Reilly, giving a dip of her head. "Can you describe the driver?"

"Yes, I think I can, but that's not the thing…"

"Go on?" said Reilly.

"When I went out, he had confronted the owner of the

BMW who was just at the edge of the woods. Neither of them looked happy to see the other, and if I'm being honest, I'd say the two of them looked to be arguing."

Chapter 7

Musgrave Street station was a modern glass and steel structure surrounded by the city's glorious past. The Police Service of Northern Ireland station was wedged between the red brick and sandstone Victorian edifice of Belfast Coroner's Court to the rear and the recently restored chromatic facade of a former ironmongery warehouse to the right. To the left lay the entrance to Victoria Square Shopping Centre and the Jaffe Fountain, the centre's glass viewing dome offering a bird's-eye view across the warren of teeming streets and entries that made up the rest of Belfast City Centre.

While it may have been a modern affair, Musgrave Street station, by the nature of its business, relied upon the remnants of a recent past for protection. The main building was surrounded by a six-foot-high double thickness concrete blast wall and above that, another twelve feet of corrugated steel enclosure was festooned with CCTV cameras to cover all routes past and provide electronic eyes for the manned security sanger on Ann Street.

Royal Irish Constabulary constables who would have stabled their horses and worked out of the old barracks a hundred years before would no doubt marvel at the metamorphosis; so too might they be amazed at how much of the old city and the old tensions remained. The unresolved political and social pressures that plagued the northeast of the isle at times still violently erupted across a city where the distinguished past remained very much in its own battle against the onslaught of modernity.

"Well, isn't that just a weeker?" said Macpherson, leaning back his chair and rolling his eyes. "Your man's vanished into thin air and while I'm out chasing shadows to the point my stomach thinks my throat's been cut, you two are twitching."

"Have you seen this though?" said Walker, pointing an RSPB sponsorship form at his sergeant. Reilly chuckled into her tea, unsure if her partner's enthusiasm for his recent excursion into the city nature reserve was genuine or had been heavily influenced by the willowy Laura Roberts.

"I don't need to go to Drumkeen Forest to see a couple of tits, son," grumbled Macpherson, dropping the front legs of the chair to the floor as Veronica Taylor entered conference room 4.12 to join her team. The inspector paused briefly, holding the door and receiving a comment of thanks from DC Carrie Cook who trailed behind.

"What's the craic with you?" said Cook, setting her laptop on the long table and proceeding to hook it up via a long USB cable to the large-screen monitor that dominated the wall.

"Peter Pecker here is channelling his inner Attenborough," said Macpherson.

Cook smiled as her fingers rattled across the keyboard. Room 4.12 was one of the dedicated meeting rooms set aside for team briefings and, on occasion, for informal interviews. The floor-to-ceiling windows looked out over Ann Street and east towards the Queen Elizabeth Bridge, the Lagan Weir and beyond that, the famous Belfast shipyard and its twin cranes, Samson and Goliath.

"I'm ready, Guv," said Cook. Taylor nodded her thanks and flicked back a few pages in her notes.

"Right, let's see what we're looking at. Do you want to kick off Carrie?" said Taylor.

"Adrian Quinn. Age thirty-four. Bladon Manor, Malone. Call received through triple nine this morning at seven forty-eight am, made by his wife, Aoife Quinn. Mrs Quinn reports her husband is incommunicado. He didn't make it to his place of work and hasn't been seen nor spoken to in twenty-four hours."

Taylor nodded her thanks.

"Doc and I visited Mrs Quinn this morning. As to be expected, she's climbing the walls. The couple have three young children and Mr Quinn going off the radar is completely out of character. Professional man, well liked and stable home life. Carrie?"

Cook dragged the mirror image of her laptop screen to the wall monitor. Taylor flipped through her notes as the DC continued.

"Adrian Quinn. Managing partner of Helios Sustainable," The screen showed the company website and a picture of the man himself, stood with an earnest expression and wearing a hi-vis jacket in a field of solar panels. The banner across the top extolled the Helios mission to empower communities with its safe and affordable renewable energy products while committing itself to engaging in the fight against climate change through innovation and technology.

"Are we sure he was on a run and wasn't down there hugging trees and done himself a mischief?" Macpherson rustled through his jacket pockets, came up empty handed, and scowled at the screen.

"Did you get out the wrong side of the bed again?" said Cook, drawing a smirk from Reilly, as she added another window to the screen to show the younger detective's snapshots of Adrian Quinn's abandoned car.

"I'm only after saying. I could eat the decorations off a hearse. You know we missed our tea rushing back here."

"And the sooner we're all on the same page, the sooner you can get to Butlers and work on your heart attack," said Taylor. Macpherson put up his hands in surrender, and Taylor continued. "We met Mr Quinn's business partner this morning. He confirms Quinn didn't arrive at work, and he's as surprised as anyone regarding the disappearance."

"I'd go as far as to say if we hadn't been called to look for him, we'd have been called to scrape him off his drive. Your man Mahood was raging, whatever the craic is," added Macpherson.

"Mr Mahood's grievance seems to stem from trouble with investors. Helios, according to Aoife Quinn, were in the process of an expansion deal. She mentioned some tension between Quinn and Mahood on the specifics of the negotiations but what I gleaned from Mahood's rant was that the deal has hit the scuppers and something Adrian Quinn has said is behind the derailment." Taylor paused, taking a sip of water. "Mahood wasn't for elaborating this morning but Doc and I have an appointment with the general manager of Helios Sustainable this afternoon to glean a bit more background."

"If the deal has broken down irrevocably, then it might be a reason for Quinn to go to ground," said Cook.

"Aye, and it might be a reason to put him there. Mahood was talking millions so cocking up might have consequences," said Macpherson.

"Chris, Erin?" Taylor pointed at the image of Quinn's car.

"Guv," Reilly shifted forward in her seat. "BMW i8, registered to Mr Quinn and reported abandoned in Drumkeen Forest Park. There was no sign of forced entry but the damage to the driver's side looks malicious."

Cook homed in on the long ragged scar.

"Ms Laura Roberts confirms Quinn as a regular visitor to the park and that she could place him there yesterday morning but she didn't see him leave."

"What time was this?" said Taylor.

"Approximately eight am."

"Which lines up with what the missus is saying," agreed Macpherson.

"Laura reported another vehicle on scene. A jeep. It blockaded Quinn's car and then he and the driver had an altercation," blurted Walker.

"Laura, now is it?" said Macpherson with a sly wink. Walker flushed.

"Ms Roberts, sarge. Sorry, Guv… I…"

"Pay him no heed, Chris. What kind of altercation?" said Taylor, with a look and a half shake of the head at her grinning sergeant.

"Initially she said it was verbal, and reading between the lines as she described it, I'd hazard a guess the two men knew each other." Reilly jerked her chin to Cook, who selected another file from the database.

"This is CCTV from the RSPB building. It's not very good but you can see Quinn arriving, then shortly afterwards, a second vehicle. Looks like a dark Range Rover, but the quality isn't good enough to get a plate and the camera covering the parking bay and the path beyond was useless."

Cook had hit the play icon and the grainy black-and-white image of Quinn's distinctive coupe, followed shortly by the other vehicle, played in jittery time-lapse.

"Ms Roberts said the verbal turned into a scuffle. She went inside to get one of the groundsmen for assistance, but when they returned the unidentified male was back in his car and reversing off. She reports seeing Quinn resume his run," said Reilly.

"Did she get a description?" Macpherson peered at the image as Cook spun back frame by frame.

"IC One male, mid to late thirties, shaven head. Not much

more."

"Could be Mahood. He has a buzz cut, and he drives a Land Rover," said Macpherson.

"I'm not sure if that's the same model, and you can't tell the colour," said Taylor. "Play it through again for us, Carrie."

Cook hit play, and the five watched first Quinn's and then the mystery car roll down the single tarmac track overshadowed by tall trees and pass across a cattle grid before disappearing from view.

"Carrie, let's assume Quinn came from his home along Malone and then onto the A55 ring. Can you access traffic cameras between Drumkeen Drive and the Minnowburn Road junction and see if ANPR caught him?" said Taylor, her mind tracing the most direct route from Quinn's home at Bladon Manor and the forest park.

"Let me try. Say between seven thirty and eight am?"

Taylor nodded and Cook began a short process of logging remotely into the traffic incident control centre. A few minutes later she had isolated the appropriate gantry cameras covering the dual carriageway that encircled the south of the city. "Call me out the reg, Chris," said Cook. Walker obliged and a minute later she had an image of the coupe travelling north toward the Drumkeen Estate. A few seconds after that she caught the 4x4.

"He's flagging him down," murmured Walker. The team watched the footage as the coupe was trailed by the bigger vehicle, its lights flashing as it aggressively drove through the morning traffic to latch onto the tail of Quinn's BMW.

"Bingo," said Cook, freezing the frame as the second of the two cars turned left into the estate and towards the entrance of the park. She switched tasks to run a vehicle PNC check on the registration now caught on screen, and waited patiently for a result. "Dark blue Ford Everest. No markings. Vehicle comes back to a Raymond Kilburn. Flat 3C Drumkeen Walk."

Macpherson hissed out a breath. Cook raised her eyes from the keyboard to look at Taylor. The inspector had a crease between her eyebrows as she studied the image on screen, searching the blur of the windshield for the face behind the wheel.

"Raymie Kilburn is known to us. He's got form for theft, minor assault and extortion, and he's on the fringes of the local paramilitary gang that operates out of the Drumkeen Estate. We suspect he's involved in loan sharking for them. Chasing up debts, meting out punishments for non-payments, all that good stuff."

"Why would he be chasing Adrian Quinn into the forest for a barney though?" said Walker, the question as much to himself as anybody else. Macpherson harrumphed.

"That's what you're going to have to ask him, son." He pointed at the image of Kilburn that Cook had dragged up from his e-record. "But keep your wits about you while you're doing it because that bugger would steal the eye out of your head."

Chapter 8

For a future-facing company engaged in fast-paced technological advancements and innovation, the premises of Helios Sustainable was, when viewed down the narrow approach road on the Forest Hill Industrial Estate, distinctly underwhelming.

The warehouse and industrial unit was sprawling, taking up the entire southern end of the small industrial park with office and production facilities comprising drab grey brickwork topped by lime green cladding. The entire compound was surrounded by a galvanised anti-climb perimeter fence and dotted with CCTV cameras.

There was no gatehouse so Taylor drove the Vauxhall straight through the open gate, following a sign which pointed to a dozen free visitor spots.

"Looks like Mr Personality is here right enough," said Macpherson, crunching down on a cinnamon lozenge and pointing to Jackie Mahood's Discovery. The vacant spot beside it was marked by a brushed stainless steel sign bearing the name of Mr A. Quinn, Director.

"It's a bit more dilapidated than I thought it would be," said Taylor, cutting the ignition and unfastening her seatbelt.

"It's what's on the inside that counts, Ronnie. Have I taught you nothing," said Macpherson with a wink, pocketing the remainder of his sweets and stepping out into the forecourt.

Helios' double entrance doors were framed by two large potted conifers and beyond the glass, they could see a more modern reception area than the outside gave credit for. Macpherson had paused a few metres ahead of the car and as Taylor turned to blip the locks, both turned their heads to raised voices as the front doors opened.

"You tell that to your solicitor, Jackie. I'll see you in court."

"You're damn right, you will. I'll have you for every penny, you two-faced bitch," snapped Jackie Mahood. He held the door open and glared after the retreating woman, tie loosened and shirt sleeves rolled up. Both antagonists had faces like smacked backsides and sensing the presence of others the woman bit back a further retort and hefted the box she carried higher in her arms, angling off to the right towards a silver Mercedes.

Mahood watched her go with a sour look of contempt on his face.

"You better not be here to torture me. I told you this morning to make an appointment," he said, shifting slightly to bar the police officers entrance while keeping an eye on the Mercedes which gunned to life and roared out the gate, a spray of gravel and trail of exhaust in its wake.

"Anybody would think you're avoiding us, sir?" said Taylor with a smile.

"I'm up to my bloody eyes so I am."

"So your PA said. We're here to see Richard Seawright." Taylor waited patiently to see if Mahood would relinquish the threshold. He grunted.

"Any sign of that other waste of space?"

"If you mean Mr Quinn, then no. Not yet, sir," said Taylor.

"Jackie? Margaret's just told me you sent Kate home…" Behind Mahood, another man was badging through the reception turnstile. He caught himself as he saw the visitors.

"They're all yours, Dicky," said Mahood, letting the door go. Macpherson caught the brushed steel handle in a big fist. "And Kate won't be coming back. I'll be in my office."

Richard Seawright looked from the faces of the two police officers to his boss's retreating back, swallowing a few times to take in the sudden pronouncement.

"Mr Seawright, Detective Inspector Taylor. This is DS Macpherson." Her voice seemed to break the spell and Seawright nodded, bidding their entry into the reception proper.

"Sorry about that. He's under some serious pressure."

Taylor watched as Mahood graced the top step of a wide floating stairway, glancing back over the balustrade towards her for a moment before breaking the look and striding on. There was a nip of stress to his features certainly, and that could be expected given the weight of responsibility for the business having been thrust solely upon him, but there remained a brash and bullish bravado that had been apparent earlier that day; it was one of the tells that piqued her senses. Her job was to investigate crime, uncover its perpetrators and bring them to book and Taylor did that ninety per cent of the time by following the evidence, which was unequivocal, and by reading people. She had arrested and charged enough individuals portraying the same demeanour over the course of her career to know Jackie Mahood was hiding something. A front of arrogance or incredulity always came first, more often than not giving way to anger and then to quiet resignation as the truth was pulled thread by thread from the chaotic tapestry of an investigation until finally, like the denouement of a magician's trick, all was revealed and then in quiet resignation the suspect would lay out mitigation for their crime while their solicitor started bargaining.

How long any of that took varied, but Taylor knew she

would get there in the end. If Seawright was correct and Mahood was under pressure, then he would make mistakes and she would be there to pick them apart and confront him, but for the moment, she couldn't be sure whether those would lead to the location of Adrian Quinn or something else entirely.

❖❖❖

"I told you not to judge a book by its cover," Macpherson wrapped his big hands around the two-inch galvanised steel tubing that formed a safety railing at the edge of the gantry where they stood overlooking the Helios production area. He gave a quiet whistle of admiration and to his left Richard Seawright smiled, his chest inflated with pride at the stunned expressions of the two detectives.

"What exactly are we looking at?" said Taylor, nodding appreciatively at the hustle of gowned and masked employees fervently beavering away at their workstations, the gleaming area below reminding her more of a sterile hospital environment than a manufacturing facility.

"This is a final testing area. Once we have established the cells perform as expected and comply with industry standards they move into the final phase of cleaning and defect inspection beyond those curtains." Seawright pointed a finger towards a set of heavy rubber crash barriers that segregated the test bay from the area beyond.

Taylor skim read the framed promotional material set at strategic intervals along the walkway. The info dumps were a means to showcase the impressive set-up Helios had established, and to educate and inform those who took the factory tour be they school children, paying customers, or canny investors.

"Hard to believe it's just sand," said Taylor, turning again to look down on the army of testers.

"Essentially." Seawright laughed. "Silicone really, which is the main component of beach sand. Given seventy per cent of the earth is covered in water it makes it the second most abundant resource on the planet."

"You must have some squad down on Portstewart stand with their buckets and spades, Mr Seawright," said Macpherson, shaking his head.

The plant manager chuckled again, relishing the opportunity to regale someone else with his passion.

"Each of the photovoltaic panels is crafted precisely and soldered together in our manufacturing area. The cells are then integrated into our patented matrix frame, which we offer to market. Our most common being the sixty-cell but we are seeing an uptake in our forty-eight-cell residential frame as well as the larger seventy-two-cell. You have to be looking for it but if you're travelling up the M2 towards Antrim you can see one of our first solar farm installations. The site was formerly twenty acres of arable farmland, and the land and the installation cost five million pounds but when you consider it will generate the owners half a million a year in energy surplus, you can see the investment potential, and that's before subsidies."

"Daylight robbery," said Macpherson, stony faced and taking the offered chair next to Taylor.

"We're making money while the sun shines, sergeant, of that there is no doubt," said Seawright with a grin. He had ensconced himself behind a utilitarian desk. The walls of his office were decorated with technical drawings of the Helios PV system and hi-res promotional photographs of deployed equipment along with a few of himself, Jackie Mahood, and Adrian Quinn at a business awards event. The centrepiece of the wall behind Seawright was a prestigious looking scroll proclaiming Helios Sustainable as winner of the Renewable Energy Innovation Design Award. A matching laser cut glass trophy sat on the desk.

"Who's that?" said Taylor, pointing out a photograph of the three men and two women.

Seawright's grin died.

"You mean the lady on the left? That's Katherine Clark."

"That's who we just saw leave, yes?" said Taylor, returning her gaze to Seawright. Never one to miss and hit the wall, she had decided on broaching the uncomfortable subject as soon as the opportunity arose.

"It is," Seawright winced. "It's unfortunate, and I expect temporary. I'm sure Jackie will calm down given time."

"Calm down? That man? If you don't mind me saying, he looks like he's fit for a stroke," said Macpherson.

"Who is she?" said Taylor. Seawright glanced at the picture, evidently taken during happier times.

"Kate is Adrian's PA. The other woman is Margaret Dawes, Jackie's. That was the night we won highly commended at the Irish Energy Awards."

"Has she been dismissed?" said Taylor, frowning.

"It's complicated."

"Mr Seawright, you've just spent half an hour explaining irradiance, power output and temperature tolerances." Taylor raised a brow and sat a bit straighter. Seawright let out a breath. "Is it to do with Mr Quinn's disappearance?" she asked, offering a route into the conversation.

Seawright nodded, then abruptly stood and strode to the window, cracking it open a few inches before returning to his seat. His cheeks were flushed.

"We are working on a fairly aggressive expansion. We have plans to triple our production capacity with the building of another plant and we've also secured locations to establish a further four solar farms, which had been granted approval by the office of regional development and would have allowed us to operate carbon neutral as well as generate a significant return of spare capacity to the grid."

"Would have?" said Taylor. Seawright nodded slowly.

"There was a meeting scheduled to finalise the plans with the department of regional development, the planning service NI and our investors but unfortunately it was hijacked."

"Sorry, you've lost me now?"

"An environmental protest group got wind of our expansion plans and set up a picket outside. The meeting was deferred and subsequently, a formal notice of complaint has been lodged with the minister of infrastructure and a planning breach submitted to the council."

"I thought the tree huggers would be lining up to hang garlands around your necks?" said Macpherson, his face creased in confusion. Taylor gave the leg of his chair a kick. Seawright shook his head sadly.

"We are committed to ensuring Northern Ireland is at the forefront of the renewable revolution and confident that our products and innovations can reduce carbon emissions and pave the way for a cleaner greener future…"

"But?" said Taylor.

"But you can't make an omelette without breaking a few eggs," said Seawright. "There is some concern, setting aside the positives of clean energy, the employment, and the reduced impact of fossil fuels, that repurposing the land will be detrimental from a conservation standpoint. Given that it's arable land, the objection is that habitat will be destroyed, the ecology of the area will suffer and that's setting to one side the impact of a two-year construction plan."

Taylor nodded slowly, beginning to understand.

"Mr Mahood thinks Katherine Clark blew the whistle."

Seawright nodded.

"Better than that, he had IT check her hard drive, and he found an email."

"But surely she understood the benefits?" said Macpherson.

"You would think so, sergeant."

"What did Mr Quinn say?" asked Taylor.

"Defended Kate to the hilt, as could be expected," said Seawright, the last uttered in an undertone.

"What do you mean by that?"

"Adrian argued she was entitled to hold an opinion and was confident that the issues could be argued away when judged against the merit of the project. He claimed it was healthy to encourage debate and find ways around those initial detrimental impacts. "

"But Mr Mahood wanted her gone?"

"He did. He was very vocal about it."

"Mr Quinn won out?"

"Kate has worked *closely* with Adrian since day one," said Seawright. The emphasis wasn't lost on either detective. "Jackie bought into the firm a few years ago. Adrian had grown the firm from his shed to what you see today, but we wouldn't be looking at the future we are without Jackie. Off the record, he thinks Kate clouds Adrian's judgement and gets away with it because she has been beside him for the whole journey and gets more of a say than her position should allow."

"When did all this come to light, Mr Seawright," said Taylor.

"The planning approval meeting was to take place three days ago. Myself, Adrian and Jackie, and the Health, Safety, Quality and Environment team were to meet yesterday to formalise a response to the objections, but Adrian was a no-show and then Jackie's investment backing pulled out. I suppose I have to say at the minute, it all looks quite bleak."

Taylor sat back and turned her attention to the photograph of the smiling faces. She couldn't help but agree. It did look bleak, for the company's grand plan, Katherine Clark's immediate employment future and most of all for the missing

Adrian Quinn.

Chapter 9

"Uh-huh?"

Raymond Kilburn stood framed in the opening of his front door. He was as described and fitted the caricature of the hard man to a T.

A receding hairline was clipped back to the scalp, leaving a fine suede of dark five o'clock shadow, and his face told the tale of too many scraps. His nose was flattened and a heavy bovine brow overhung puffy brown eyes, with evidence of a more recent incident glaringly obvious by the plaster over his right eyebrow and a blooming black eye beneath.

A tattoo of a pair of red lips kissed the right-hand side of his thick neck, which rolled into broad muscled shoulders and a barrel chest squeezed into a regulation two sizes too small black tee shirt. From inside the flat came the snarling bark of at least two dogs.

"Raymond Kilburn?" said Walker, forcing his voice an octave lower and pulling back his shoulders.

"You knocked the door, who were you looking for?" Kilburn nonchalantly leaned against the frame, crossing one ankle behind the other.

"DC Reilly. DC Walker. Do you have five minutes for a chat?" Reilly held out her warrant card, looking over Kilburn's shoulder to the hallway beyond.

"I didn't know you lot were doing social calls? You'll be wanting tea and custard creams next?"

"Do you mind if we come inside?" said Reilly.

"Do you not need a warrant for that?" Kilburn smiled, the movement doing little to soften his features.

"Do we need one?"

Kilburn chuckled and rolled his eyes. "Hang on a minute."

Before either of the detectives could speak, Kilburn slammed the door closed, the black knocker rattling hard against the PVC and setting off another series of loud barks from inside. Walker quickly stepped back down the steps towards a path that led around the side of the flats.

"Where are you going?" Reilly spun around as Walker dug in his jacket for his TETRA radio. The look on his face said he wasn't taking the chance their lead was flying the coop.

The front door opened again. Kilburn, taken aback at only seeing Reilly, moved to peer past her to a stuttering Walker.

"Did you think I was doing a runner or something? You lot have no faith in people. Come on in."

The hallway was gloomy but clean and a plug-in air fresher was winning the battle with the whiff of damp dog. The offender, barks having died to a low grumble, was peering over a child safety gate fastened across the kitchen door. Kilburn turned right into the lounge, flopping down on an armchair.

"I should thank you really," he said, gesturing to the television. "You've saved me from listening to that lot drone a load of shite." The TV was tuned to an afternoon magazine show, the panel discussing the day's current affairs, celebrity gossip and showbiz news. He muted the cackling presenters and gestured to the sofa. The lounge was bright and overlooked the main road where the dark blue Ford Explorer was parked. Beyond, a wall of trees could be seen on the other side of four flat football pitches bisected by the driveway into Drumkeen Forest Park.

The arm of Kilburn's chair and the laminate floor had lost the battle to the dog, scratches and teeth marks having been gouged from the edges of each.

"Did you think you were going to find the place stacked with gear?" said Kilburn clocking Walker's observations. The DC blushed.

"So, to what do I owe the pleasure?" said Kilburn.

Erin Reilly pulled out her notebook and shuffled forward on her seat.

"Is that your car down there, Mr Kilburn?"

"You're the detective, love."

"We're investigating an incident over at the forest yesterday," said Reilly. Kilburn sniffed, a hand unconsciously going to the plaster over his eye then dropping back to the arm of the chair.

"Oh aye, what's it to do with me?"

"Do you recognise this man?" Walker held up his mobile phone, the screen displaying a picture of Adrian Quinn in a business suit.

Kilburn's lips twisted, but he didn't reply.

"He's missing," said Reilly.

"Again, what's that got to do with me." Kilburn shrugged. He had retrieved the remote control for the TV and bounced it off the fabric of his chair.

"ANPR cameras on the carriageway show your car flashing its lights and driving aggressively to intercept another vehicle." Reilly jerked her head in the direction of the A55. "Cameras from the forest park drive show you tailed the vehicle to the parking area and an eye witness places a man fitting your description and this man in an argument."

"Couldn't be much of an eye witness," mumbled Kilburn with a shake of the head, an expression of annoyance flashing across his face.

"For the record, are you saying they're mistaken?" said Reilly.

"I'm saying their eyes must be painted on."

Reilly could see agitation beginning to rise in Kilburn. The gentle tapping of the remote had turned into a slightly more aggressive stabbing motion.

"You're not denying anything then?"

"I'm not admitting to anything either," snapped Kilburn.

"I'm not asking you to admit anything, Mr Kilburn. We're trying to find a missing person and regardless of the circumstances, you may have been one of the last people to have seen him."

Kilburn paused the abuse of the remote control and looked at Reilly, his eyes narrowing.

"Do you think I'm daft? If this boy turns up dead or injured, you'll be looking at the last person to have seen him as the culprit."

"If you know that, then you know that's the likelihood," said Reilly with a shrug. "Victims either know their attacker or it's the last person to be seen in their company. Give us a reason to rub you off the list."

"I don't know him," said Kilburn.

"But?" said Walker, sensing the hesitation in the statement.

"I did have a barney with him."

"Yesterday?"

"Aye, yesterday."

"Can you tell us what it was about?"

"Oh aye, the arrogant bastard nearly killed my dog."

Reilly shared a look with Walker.

"Mr Kilburn, you chased this man along the ring road, blocked his car in and had an altercation in front of a witness. There was no mention of a dog present?" said Walker.

"That's because she's in there recovering." Kilburn stabbed a thumb towards the kitchen. "I see your man in his fancy car most days heading into the park for a run. I'm normally on my way back out with Duchess. Anyway, start of the week we were the other way about, the frigging car's electric and you don't hear it until it's on top of you. The wee dog stepped out, and he clipped her. Bastard just drove on. "

"You didn't report it?" said Walker. Kilburn laughed and looked at Reilly.

"Is he new to this?" Reilly waited on him to elaborate further. "Of course I didn't report it, sunshine. I knew the dickhead would be back and there was more chance I'd get through to him than you lot."

"Mr Kilburn, I have to warn you, taking matters into your own hands isn't a sensible option," said Reilly, marking a note in the book to review Kilburn's history in relation to section 39 assaults.

"You're telling me," said Kilburn with a huff of breath. Silence hung in the air for a beat until he shifted forward in his seat and waggled a finger at Reilly's notebook. "I hope you do find the bastard and do you know what? You're right."

Walker raised an eyebrow, shaking his head as Kilburn shifted his gaze between the two police officers.

"I want to report a hit and run and I want to report an assault."

"Mr Kilburn—" said Reilly, but Kilburn cut her off.

"You want to show me that I should keep my nose out of it and you're worth your salt, then you stick it to the bastard that did this." Kilburn jabbed two thumbs in the direction of his face.

Reilly focused on the split skin under the broad plaster and the glorious purple haze around his eye.

"Your missing man smashed me in the face with a bloody big log. I know you've been sitting there thinking I'm the one with the history of violence but have you even took the time to look past his fancy car and bloody three-piece suit?"

When neither detective responded, Kilburn sighed and slumped back in his chair.

"I didn't think so, but I tell you this for nothing. If he had the balls to do this to me and think nothing of the consequences, then who else has he been stupid enough to get on the wrong side of?"

Chapter 10

"I suppose it's five o'clock somewhere," said Macpherson.

Katherine Clark shook her head wearily and set her glass beside an uncorked bottle of Dönnhoff Riesling. Taylor, entering the open-plan lounge behind her detective sergeant, noted by the remaining contents that it wasn't her first tipple of the day.

"Obviously, I'd offer you some but you're on duty," said Clark.

"By the look of things you've been released from your work responsibilities for the moment." Taylor jutted her chin to where the box of personal effects from her workspace at Helios sat on a stool pulled out from the breakfast bar.

Katherine Clark had piled her hair up on top of her head and divested herself of the smart check, navy two-piece suit and camel overcoat she had worn earlier in the day, to wear a pair of black skinny jeans and check shirt over a white vest top.

Double doors to a Juliette balcony at the front of the apartment were open and the hum of steady traffic threading along the main arterial route of the Lisburn Road droned in the background, competing with the melodic rhythm of pop music stemming from an Alexa device on the kitchen worktop.

Clark's apartment overlooked a block of thriving shopping outlets. Directly opposite her balcony, a queue had formed outside a Caffe Nero, and the shops, boutiques, wine bars and restaurants alongside seemed to be enjoying an equally brisk trade. The windows at the other end of the open-plan living space offered a view out over an M&S food hall and across the roofs of terraced streets to the Boucher Road and the imposing smudge of Divis and the Black Mountain beyond.

"A temporary blip," said Clark.

"You expect Adrian Quinn to be back then?" said Taylor. Clark fussed with her hair and shrugged.

"Even if he's not, Jackie Mahood will be on the phone before the week's out when he realises he hasn't a clue about anything other than his way around a profit and loss account."

"You've no idea where Adrian could be?"

"No." Clark shook her head.

"Is Adrian the type of man who keeps secrets?"

"He's the more introverted of the two but I wouldn't say secretive, no."

"Richard Seawright tells us you've been there from the start, that you worked closely with Adrian. Are you sure he never mentioned anything, gave away any hints something may be bothering him, or share any concerns?" said Taylor, taking the offered armchair as Clark moved away from the small kitchen island and sat on the sofa opposite, curling her legs underneath her.

"I bet you that's not all he bloody told you."

"Would you like to tell us your side of it?"

Clark sighed and rubbed a hand over her eyes.

"Where do you want me to start?"

"Beginning's as good as anywhere," said Macpherson, nudging down beside Taylor and offering across his packet of brandy balls which Clark declined.

"Adrian and I used to work together at an electrical contracting firm. He spotted a gap in the market for photovoltaic panels when they first came on the scene way back. He's wild for wanting to know how things work so over a few years he had pulled what was on the market apart enough times to understand there was a more efficient way of building them while improving the aesthetic and the output. He started a cottage industry out at the house and then when he moved out of the shed up to the unit he brought me across as an administration manager."

"Smart buck then, is he?" said Macpherson, crunching down on a sweet.

"More brains than he knows what to do with," agreed Clark.

"And you'd agree he's not the type to drop off the radar?"

Clark shifted as she addressed Taylor, dropping one foot to the floor.

"It's not like him, but then things had got quite heated over the last while."

"With the issues surrounding the expansion project?" said Taylor.

"Not just that. I suppose you have to understand the relationship between him and Jackie."

"They're business partners," said Macpherson, giving a stiff nod. "In cahoots to make a ton of money and from what we saw at the factory they're doing that alright."

"We *were* on track," said Clark, pursing her lips and giving a reciprocal nod.

"You were?" said Taylor.

"I mean until all this."

"And the relationship between the two partners?"

"Not what it used to be," said Clark with a shake of the head.

"Any specific reason other than the leak of the expansion

plan to the environmental group?" said Taylor. Clark's lips set in a tight line and she pressed herself back into the sofa, drawing her foot from the floor again.

"It wasn't a leak."

"I don't think that's how your boss is choosing to see it," said Macpherson.

"The thing you have to understand about Jackie is he wants the last word. It's his way or no way and Adrian was getting fed up with it." Clark abruptly stood. She moved to the kitchen island and retrieved and recharged her glass of wine, aiming it at the two detectives as she returned to her seat. "Adrian and I built that company from the ground up, there would be no business if it wasn't for him, but Jackie thinks because he bankrolled some investment that he can have the final say and he's not shy in casting up how he could take his investment and move on."

"You're saying he was strong-arming Quinn for control?" said Taylor.

"Do you not call it blackmail or something?" said Clark, taking a long sip of the Riesling.

"Blackmail only works when you have something that compromises the injured party and you're willing to leverage it for gain," said Macpherson.

"And I'm saying Jackie was threatening to reconsider his investment if Adrian didn't agree to his scope for the expansion." Clark's hand, not occupied by the glass, gesticulated to emphasise her point.

"Well, one thing's for sure the expansion and any big payday is off the table now the cat's out of the bag and you've more objections coming in than beaten dockets after the Grand National." Macpherson gave Clark a stiff nod and sat back in his seat.

"What specifically were Jackie's demands, Katherine?" said Taylor.

"He'd highlighted half a dozen sites for solar farms. Typical Jackie had beat the owners over the head with his cheque book and acquired four straight off the bat. Adrian was aware there might be cause for objection on a couple of them and wanted to thrash out a conservation plan before word got out. Jackie wanted the train to be too far out of the station to turn back. One of the sites Adrian point-blank vetoed." Clark took a sip of her wine.

"Do you know his reasons for the veto?"

"He said the land wasn't suitable, something to do with subsidence or substrate. For whatever reason Jackie wanted that tract and was willing to use the threat of pulling his shares out of the business if he couldn't have it."

"Would you be able to tell us where these sites are?" said Taylor. Clark nodded.

"It will be public record now. Three were on a crescent of agricultural land between Drumbeg and Carryduff with another inside the city limits on a patch of council-owned ground marked for redevelopment."

"Thanks, I'll take a look at them." Taylor scratched a note to research the sites and their significance, if any. She closed her notebook and set it on the arm of the sofa, appraising Clark, whose cheeks had developed a tint of rose either from the wine or her frustrations at the actions of Jackie Mahood and her sudden unemployment. "Katherine, you don't have to answer this, but did you leak the information on those proposed developments knowing it would halt progress and spite Jackie?"

Clark gave a single, silent nod.

"Publicity is a double-edged sword," said Taylor.

"One I've just fallen on." Clark gave a weak smile.

"Did Adrian Quinn ask you to release that email?"

Clark didn't nod straight away, but she did and then followed it up with a half shake that wobbled the hair piled up on her head.

"Adrian built the business and our reputation through relationships, not by steamrolling people or tying objections up in red tape. He was confident that dialogue would see the proposed production facility given the green light, and the protests assuaged by ensuring all the environmental responsibilities of the build were met and any impact offset by creating a biodiverse parkland around the factory."

"And Jackie?"

"Crunched the numbers and said an injunction would cost less in time and material."

Taylor took a breath and pondered what she had learned from the woman. Her gut told her Katherine Clark was, so far as she herself knew, telling the truth. That truth may be skewed somewhat in her loyalty to Adrian Quinn, but given what she had seen of Jackie Mahood, she couldn't argue with the label of hard-nosed businessman and bean counter. Clark interrupted her thoughts, setting the empty glass on the floor and leaning forward, eyes searching each of the detectives.

"You need to understand that's the man Aido is," said Clark. "He stands up for what he believes in. We've taken a financial hit lately but he still put people and protection of the environment above pure profit. We've had ups and downs in shifting the retail focus from fossil to renewables and this year alone we've had two suppliers tank and we'll never see our money come back. Adrian knew Helios needed this expansion to climb out of the hole, but he wasn't going to compromise on his beliefs. He hasn't made one redundancy in the lifetime of Helios and he re-mortgaged to make sure he didn't have to this time either."

"He must have been confident the gamble would pay off?" said Taylor, taking up her notebook and writing a bullet point to check Quinn's bank records.

"It wasn't a gamble to him. He knew by putting the word

out and going about addressing objections in the right way, it would pay dividends in the end."

"But he couldn't be seen to do it himself," said Taylor.

"He didn't need to do it himself. He had me, and I'd do anything he asked." Clark's tone was assured and unapologetic. Taylor snapped her notebook closed and returned it to her inside jacket pocket, setting her gaze on the woman opposite.

"Katherine, was your relationship with Adrian purely professional?"

Clark opened her mouth to deny it and then shook her head instead.

"What has that got to do with—"

"Adrian Quinn is missing, and it's my job to ensure he returns to his life safely. The reasons why he has disappeared are likely to stem from personal or professional challenges he has been facing so I'd appreciate it if you were straight with me."

"Aido wasn't just my boss, he was my best friend," said Clark, her eyes welling up as Taylor's words hit home. During the moment it took for Clark to compose herself, Taylor reassessed what she had seen of the apartment and gleaned from the woman's body language.

"Did you ever cross the line with him?"

"Was I sleeping with him?"

The two detectives waited in silence for her to answer her own question.

"Once. We slept together once, before the boys came along."

"And that was it?"

"That was it. It wasn't a mistake, it just wasn't meant to be," said Clark, her voice thickened with emotion.

"You love him, don't you?" said Taylor.

The dam of the day's emotions broke and Clark tipped her

head forward to hide the tears, but they dripped like raindrops onto her jeans.

Taylor sensed the pain of emptiness and loss radiate from the woman to saturate the fabric of the apartment which, like the owner, was delicately feminine and perhaps a bit clinical, but most apparent of all was missing the heart that would make it a home.

She opened two more mental files to sit beside the one containing financial motivations for Adrian Quinn's disappearance; the jilted lover and the scorned wife.

Chapter 11

The door to the RSPB headquarters was closed and there were no lights on inside or any sign of Laura Roberts. The overgrowing ivy seemed to have made more progress in wrapping the old stable block in its tendrils just as the area around Adrian Quinn's car and the path to the forest park's walking trail was now festooned in red and white police tape.

"We'll start with a grid around the vehicle and then work our way out."

Erin Reilly nodded, following the fingertip of the search team leader as it crossed the planned search area on an ordinance survey map spread out on the bonnet of his van.

"Great. Can I have you traverse the path to where the altercation was reported and, depending on what we find, adjust the plan from there?"

Constable Brian Butler gave his agreement with a murmured affirmative and a thumbs up, accepting Reilly's gratitude with a smile as he turned to open the back door of the Ford Transit Connect and ready his partner for action. Reilly paused as the cage was opened and as Butler readied the dog's yellow working harness. She took a moment to ruffle the floppy ears of the chocolate Labrador and accept the excited kisses as the dog waited to be put to work.

"Erin, where do you want him?"

Chris Walker stood thirty feet away from the cordoned-off BMW and gestured down the lane at an approaching vehicle recovery truck.

"Send him over there until Diane's folks have finished up." Reilly directed Walker to a gravel area of overflow parking to the far right of the car park, and as he trotted across to intercept the driver she made her way to the cordon surrounding Quinn's car.

"Don't suppose he left us a note, Di?"

Diane Pearson peered through the open passenger door from her position on haunches at the open driver's side. She gave a shake of her head as she stood, losing a strand of her ash blonde hair from the hood of her forensic Tyvek over suit; the forensic science service senior crime scene investigator tucked it back in before removing her nitrile gloves and making her way to Reilly.

"Diddley squat, Erin." Pearson removed her facemask and turned to follow Reilly's look towards the other two SOCOs who were carefully going through the rear seats, footwells, and the open boot of the BMW. "The spare key you gave us did the job of getting in. Locks and alarm were still engaged. No sign of attempted forced entry or evidence of anything other than he pulled up and got out. Suit bag was hung in the rear with a pair of brogues, and a towel and cereal bars on the front passenger seat, bin bag on the floor, probably for his mucky guddies. So, it's looking as reported. Your guy went for a run and hasn't come back."

"The damage to the side?"

Pearson shrugged.

"Broad flat object, single point of contact and I see one ridge so if you're asking me to take a punt somebody keyed it. Sorry, I've nothing more definitive but then maybe that's a good thing?"

"Yeah maybe," agreed Reilly. The suspicion that they

would open the boot to find Quinn's body had never really left her until Pearson had given the word there was no sign of violence beyond that against the polished bodywork.

"Cheers, Di, give me a shout when you're done and we'll get the lads to lift the car."

Pearson smiled and retrieved a new set of gloves from her kitbag set on the outside of the cordon.

"How's my old mate Doc doing?" she said.

"Still losing friends and alienating people," said Reilly, as Pearson's broad grin and chuckle disappeared behind her mask. "I'll give you a shout if we turn anything up, okay?"

"When we're finished here, we'll be in the van," said Pearson, turning with a wave.

Reilly met Walker halfway back to the row of police vehicles and the dog handler's van. A dozen uniforms, kitted out in rifle green waterproofs and PSNI logoed caps, stood in a loose semi-circle waiting for the off; each held a long pole to aid balance and pace the step-by-step search of the undergrowth and woodland that would be led by Brian Butler and Flynn the Lab.

"We good to go, Brian?" asked Reilly, as Butler patted the dog's neck and secreted her tennis ball in his waterproof overcoat.

"Ready when you are, Erin."

"Okay, ladies and gents. You've seen the brief. Adrian Quinn, missing, and last seen heading into the woods more than twenty-four hours ago. We've initially four search areas as per briefing pack. Alpha through Delta extending from the path intersection over there where it's reported Mr Quinn engaged in a scuffle with a man subsequently identified as Raymond Kilburn." There were a few raised eyebrows and a low murmur of recognition at the name. "Flynn will run the ground to the location and we'll be led by her and Brian. All good?"

A chorus of curt affirmatives and nods returned, and Reilly gave Butler a thumbs up. Walker, carrying a plastic evidence bag, passed it across to the dog handler who presented the contents to his partner, a white undershirt belonging to Adrian Quinn and donated by his wife for the purpose of the search. Flynn's tail whipped back and forth, her tongue lolling from a happy mouth and her paws tapping the ground in eager anticipation.

"Go find," said Butler, his voice charged with excitement and encouragement.

Flynn set off at a trot, disappearing into the knee-high grass that bordered the car park and the pathways, her tail wagging as she picked up pace, sweeping ten by ten-metre squares through the undergrowth; an occasional pause and glance back to her master who encouraged her on.

The search team spread into a long line and began the trek across the open ground towards the tree line, the bounding dog cutting a swathe ahead. Reilly and Walker followed Brian Butler in the centre of the phalanx, taking the meandering path that Quinn would have followed. Reilly caught Butler stiffen a second before she caught a change in Flynn's body language. The dog's tail had flattened and her nose had dropped. She looked up for direction.

"Good girl, Flynn. She has something," said Butler veering off the path to where his dog had ceased her methodical sweeps through the grass and was nose down in the undergrowth.

"Good girl." Butler's voice was effusive in praise, and he reached inside his coat to reward the dog with her ball. Flynn panted happily, her tail whumping against her handler's leg.

"What is it?" said Reilly, stepping forward.

"Branch."

Walker carefully eased the grass aside to reveal the arm-length stump of deadfall; on one end a darkened smear that looked like blood.

"Mark it and leave a man here. We'll give Diane the nod to collect it."

"Could be the weapon Kilburn told us about?" said Walker.

"Yep, and it will lend credence to his side of the story if it's his blood and not Quinn's." Reilly jumped at an excited bark from Flynn.

"Something else?"

"Good girl, go find," said Butler, nodding. "We're getting the wind onside, it's blowing across from the west right onto her nose."

Flynn dropped her ball and soared off like a sleek brown missile. Any methodical back-and-forth sonar sweep lost to the laser focus of a scent now caught on the breeze. She bounded through the tree line, a series of sharp barks in her wake as Butler, with Reilly and Walker in tow hurried after her.

The dog's yellow vest flitted between trees, Reilly catching sight of her scramble down a bank of heather and broadleaf ferns.

"Flynn, easy," Butler's voice was measured, his concern the dog might turn a leg on the uneven ground and jutting root systems in contrast to his partner's excited headlong charge.

The police officers scrambled down the bank, Reilly clutching at the mossy bark of broad oaks and elms to ease her descent as Walker slip-slided gracelessly away to her right. They crashed into a small clearing at the bottom of the slope at the same time. The ripple of water and the quack of wildfowl signified their proximity to the meandering River Lagan a little further ahead through the trees.

Flynn was frozen stock still on the boundary of the clearing, her eyes darting to her handler, but her nose pointed to a patch of overgrown shrubbery in the understory of the forest canopy.

"Good girl, Flynn. Great job." Butler gave his dog her ball, and Reilly patted the excited animal as she got close.

Shoved in amongst the leaves and the deadfall was a stuffed black bin liner. At some point in the bag's journey down the slope it had split and, on impact, some of its contents had spilled out, amongst them a single muddied ASICS running shoe and an orange Under Armour vest.

"Call it in, Chris," said Reilly, ruffling the dog's ears. "You've some nose on you, girl."

Flynn's big brown eyes looked between Reilly and a red-faced but chuffed Brian Butler. She dropped her ball at Reilly's feet and woofed her impatience for another game of go find Adrian Quinn.

Chapter 12

"It's just hit me you know, I'm some mentor." Macpherson pulled the Volvo up kerbside, puffed with pride and in absent-minded satisfaction he tried to rip off the handbrake.

"Self-praise is no recommendation, Doc," said Taylor with a chuckle as she unfastened her seat belt.

"Aye, credit where credit is due you've some eyes on you, but I'm telling you, you must have fair soaked up some expertise from me over the years."

"You should put in for the training college. Think of all those recruits you could mould into wee carbon copies." Taylor exited the car as a horrified look broke on her sergeant's face at the thought. "But let me know when you take the notion to the chief super. I want to be there to see his face at the thought of that."

Across the entranceway of the Quinn property, Leigh-Anne Arnold's Škoda patrol car remained parked.

"Ma'am." Arnold lowered the driver's window as Taylor and Doc approached.

"Leigh-Anne, all quiet?" said Taylor, leaning down with a hand on the roof.

"Mrs Quinn hasn't gone out. Her mother came back with the kids about an hour ago. No other visitors."

"No press or anything hanging about?" Arnold shook her

head.

Taylor pursed her lips and gave the constable a nod. The reports had gone out to the radio and television networks appealing for witnesses in and around Drumkeen Forest Park alongside a description of Adrian Quinn and his suspected route the morning of his disappearance. So far nothing had come from it but if the investigation did segue down a darker path Arnold and her colleagues would have a job of it keeping the vultures from the Quinns' gate.

"We've a few things to run past Mrs Quinn. Sign us into the log there, will you?"

"Will do, ma'am."

Walking to the high automatic gate, Macpherson thumbed the intercom as Taylor took in the expanse of the property and that of its neighbours. Bladon Manor was a desirable address in a leafy upmarket suburb and if Helios had been clipped by a few suppliers going belly up and the expansion deal going sour, cash flow was going to be a problem and there was nothing like the notion of losing your fancy home to twist the thumbscrews on marital bliss.

There was a brief crackled exchange and then the gates began to hum open. The two police officers entered, taking the narrow brick path up towards the house.

"Final demands?" said Macpherson, shaking his head. "I could barely read the date on the milk."

"I didn't think much of it at the time and she said she was looking for a note from Adrian. I noticed two piles of paperwork, the bigger stack was all bank and insurance related. I clocked at least two demand notices," said Taylor, thinking back to their previous visit.

Aside from the Porsche which hadn't moved, there was a Mercedes E-Class estate nudged up on the turning circle near the edge of the lawn. So far no one had come to the entrance porch to welcome the visitors. "Based on what Katherine

Clark said about re-mortgaging to shore up the factory I'm wondering why Aoife Quinn didn't come clean and tell us they had money problems."

"You wouldn't think it to look at this place," said Macpherson, again running an appreciative eye across the landscaped gardens.

"You hardly ever do." Taylor had just reached the porch steps when Aoife Quinn opened the door.

"Inspector? Have you…" Her question died on her lips, wanting to ask but not really wanting to know the answer.

"No, Mrs Quinn, we have no news yet. I just wanted to follow up with a few more questions."

"Okay, come in. Excuse the mess, the kids are back and they go through the place like a whirlwind."

There was no mess that Taylor could lay her eye on, but somewhere upstairs she heard the tinkle of childish laughter and thud of small feet.

"It's the police, Mum. This is my mum Caroline."

Aoife's mother had shared her fine bone structure with her daughter, and although she offered a warm smile, the tension around her eyes didn't lift.

"Any news?"

"Sorry, ma'am. We are recovering Adrian's car now and have a few leads to follow up but nothing concrete," said Taylor. Then turning to Aoife. "No word here? No calls?" Quinn had backed up against the worktop. The telephone handset was in its cradle to the right of her elbow, blinking alerts to missed calls. Aoife shook her head. She looked ready for tears.

"Would you mind if we sat down?" said Taylor.

"Tea?" said Caroline Quinn.

Taylor shook her head, Macpherson following her lead and for once declining a second polite query when asked were they sure.

"I'll go and make sure the kids don't interrupt you."

"Thanks, Mum. Please." Quinn offered them the same seats as before. The only difference was a few of the morning tabloids had been skimmed through and left open on the coffee table. A pen lay on the open page of the classifieds section.

"Did you speak to Jackie?" said Quinn. She sat on the edge of her chair, knees together, feet apart and palms clamped between her thighs.

"We spoke to a manager at Helios, Richard Seawright. We'll be going back to speak with Mr Mahood after this."

Quinn's eyes dropped away, a look akin to relief crossing her face.

"We also had a conversation with Katherine Clark," said Taylor softly.

"Oh." Mention of the name prickled across Quinn's expression, hardening it, and the single syllable came out through clenched teeth.

"Mr Seawright told us she's a fixture at Helios and a long term colleague of your husband?"

"Why don't you just spit it out, Inspector." Quinn's eyes narrowed and she sat back with crossed arms. "Did I know about my husband's affair with her? Yes, I did. He told me and I forgave him. Anything she thinks she knows about what's going on with Aido you can take with a pinch of salt." As she spoke, the tremble of emotion built in her words.

"She didn't have any information that might lead us to where Adrian is but she did mention some recent financial impacts suffered by Helios."

Quinn gave a half shrug.

"When does a business ever run smoothly? It's not like the administrators are at the door, is it? With Jackie's investment and getting the expansion deal back on track, it will be a storm in a teacup. Katherine Clark likes people to think she's more important to the running of the company than she really is."

Taylor took out her notebook and made a show of reviewing a few points. She was sure Quinn's explanation was one that Adrian had drummed into his wife when she had asked similar questions.

"You looking to get rid of a few things?" Taylor jutted her chin at the classified ads and Quinn blushed.

"Some of Sophie's stuff; prams, trampoline, the things she never uses anymore. You know anybody?"

"She's a bit big for a pram and the bouncing would kill my old knees," said Macpherson with a sympathetic smile and a nod to Taylor.

"Mrs Quinn, are you having trouble financially?" said Taylor.

"No," said Quinn. "Not really."

"I couldn't help but notice the statements—" Taylor was cut off by the phone ringing. Quinn sprang to her feet and grabbed the handset.

"Aido?"

"Hello? For God's sake!"

Taylor stood as Quinn jabbed the call end button and tossed the handset onto the counter.

"Mrs Quinn?"

"It's nothing. Stupid kids or something."

"How long have you been getting them?"

Quinn beckoned Taylor to sit and flopped back down in her armchair.

"A while. Adrian said to ignore them."

"Did he give any indication if he knew who it might be?"

"No. Well, he said it might be people with a grudge against the new work. You heard about the environmental protestors?"

"Do they ever speak?" said Taylor, nodding to indicate that

they had been informed of the complaint and protest.

Quinn shook her head. She was hunched over and tense and began to bite the thumbnail of her right hand. "No, not a word."

"We'll look into it, okay?" said Taylor. Quinn didn't respond.

"The bank statements, and maybe these calls? Did Adrian borrow money?"

"No." The words were out before Taylor had finished.

"I'm going to run a credit report and find out, Aoife. It'd be easier if you gave me a heads-up on what I'll find?"

Quinn put her head in her hands.

"Okay. Okay. Yes, we're up to our necks in it all thanks to my wonderful husband."

Taylor nodded and waited for her to carry on.

"Saint Aido. Never let anyone down in his life. He'll go without, so everyone else gets what they're due. It's a pity he never thought what that would mean for his bloody children."

"How bad is it?"

"It's worse now I don't know where Aido is and Jackie is telling me this expansion project that was to put everything back on track is ruined."

"You must have a few quid in the bank though?" said Macpherson. Quinn snorted.

"Aido had to plough everything he could into Helios. His pride couldn't see him upstaged by Jackie, even though he was the firm. There wouldn't be a business without his drive and technical ability or the loyalty of the staff to him."

"When did he tell you he had re-mortgaged the house?"

"He didn't; I found out by accident."

"Do you think he might have had reason to borrow elsewhere as well?"

"No... I don't know." Quinn threw up an exasperated

hand. "All I know is he's missing and I want him home. I don't care about the bloody house or the stupid money, I want the kids to have their daddy back."

Taylor heard a genuine plea in Quinn's voice and felt a stab of sympathy for the woman. She had aged a few years in the time since they had met and clearly hadn't slept or found time for a minute's peace. She seemed adrift amid the mod-cons of the lavish house and its expansive gardens. As their eyes met, she felt sympathy rise to pity and had the same overwhelming sensation that she had felt in Katherine Clark's apartment, that feeling of a house missing the joy and beating heart that made it a home.

"What are you thinking?"

"I'm thinking she's in the dark as much as us and I'm thinking Aido Quinn might be in bigger bother than we thought?" said Taylor.

Macpherson gunned the Volvo across the Newforge Lane junction, habitually glancing to his left down the tree-lined road that led to the PSNI Sports and Social Club and memories of many a heady night and a heavy head.

"Dodgy loans?"

"Raymie Kilburn. He's the last person to be seen with Quinn and we know he's a shark for the hoods in Drumkeen Estate," said Taylor, nodding.

Macpherson weaved into the left lane and took an inside racing line around the House of Sport roundabout heading south on the A55 back towards Drumkeen Forest and the Forest Hill Industrial Estate.

"You bringing him in?"

Taylor shook her head and reached for her mobile, thumbing open the home screen and placing a call.

"Carrie? It's me... yeah, not so bad. Do me a favour, we've just come from the Quinn house and they've been receiving nuisance phone calls. Have a check through the telecoms company and see if we can find the source."

Taylor waited as Carrie Cook replied.

"Approximately half an hour ago while we were there, and probably over the last few weeks. Do the needful on a credit check for Quinn too. It looks like he's in a bit of bother... Yeah, we were just talking about Kilburn..." Cook's query was identical to Macpherson's.

"No, not until we see the extent of the debts or unless Erin and Chris get something. We're going to Helios to see Jackie Mahood here, so I've one last thing. I'm going to text you a few addresses linked to the Helios expansion deal. Run them down and see if there's anything out of the ordinary about them. Cheers, Carrie, we'll see you in a bit."

Taylor closed the call just as Macpherson hit the first traffic calming measure on the road up to Helios Sustainable. As their progress slowed to negotiate the humps and the building loomed ahead she could see the car park had emptied as was to be expected for the time of day. Thankfully, the big green Discovery was still parked where it had been earlier.

"Who let you in?"

"You're a man after my own heart," said Macpherson, pointing at the thick-bottomed tumbler containing an inch of whiskey that sat beside a glass decanter.

"Not a bad time, is it?" said Taylor, receiving the expected scowl from Jackie Mahood.

"Sit yourselves down and make it quick if you can."

Mahood swivelled his high-backed chair and slid out from behind his desk, picking up the tumbler and taking a swig. Swirling the liquid around in his mouth before he swallowed, he took a satisfied breath.

"Hope you're not planning on driving home?" said

Macpherson, taking the seat to Taylor's right.

"I'll be lucky to be out of here tonight," grunted Mahood. "That wee shite's left some mess behind him."

"Do you want to elaborate?" said Taylor, easing into the plush visitor's chair and crossing her legs.

"Fuck sake, are you serious. Do you want me to tell you about how he squandered a couple of hundred grand of my money on a new inverter I told him would never work or how that other bitch shafted me to the green gang?"

"I thought it was the business's money?"

Mahood hissed a tut and turned to look out of the floor-to-ceiling window behind him. On the other side of the glass, the factory was dark, bathed in pools of low light from LED bulkheads and overhead spot, the workforce having trickled out a few hours earlier.

"Aye, well. It is. It was. But it was only there to spend because of me." He thumbed over his shoulder towards the rows of darkened workstations. "Where do you think that came from? The fairies sure as hell didn't bring it."

"Was there a bit of a power struggle going on, Mr Mahood?" said Taylor.

"Tug of war more like."

"I see…"

"No, you don't." Mahood turned back and collected his glass. "You think I'm an overbearing arrogant prick and you'd be right. That how I ended up with the cash to fund Aido's passion project."

"You must have seen some worth to stump up?" said Macpherson.

"I'm not daft, renewable is the future." Mahood aimed the glass at the two officers. "Now, I'm not on my save the planet high horse here, it's just good business to get in on the ground floor, and to be fair to him, Aido knew what he was about."

"So, what's with the tug of war?" said Taylor. "Did you not want the same thing in the end?"

"I thought we did. To get stinking rich and make a bit of a difference while we're at it. It made a change to the cut and thrust I was used to."

"Which was?"

"The City. Investment banking. It didn't matter two hoots about what we bought or sold, or the impact those trades had out on the ground or in the long term, as long as the stock dividends went up. This was different. Aido was on to a winner and, played right, Helios could be a market leader."

Taylor tapped her foot as she considered Mahood, his candour and his nod to having a continued belief Helios could move him past whatever grievances the two directors were having at present.

"What do you think's going on with Adrian's disappearance?" she said. Mahood took another sip of his drink and held the liquid in his mouth as he pondered. He swallowed.

"Look, you're coppers, not entrepreneurs but you're not stupid. Aido's been throwing good money after bad and I had to stop him before he sent ten years of his own hard work and a few million of my money down the drain."

"And how did you go about that, sir?" Macpherson slid forward on his chair and gave Mahood a steely glare.

"Like any responsible parent. I gave him a stern word and threatened to take his bloody bank card off him." Mahood sat. "Look, what we need as a company is to stick to what we know. What we are good at. The manufacture and installation of PV panels. The product is sound, affordable, tried and tested. Aido was trying to get the next generation off the ground before the bloody market had embraced the first. It was suicide."

"That's an interesting interpretation," said Taylor, noticing

Macpherson stiffen at the mention of the word.

"You know what I mean. Look, I don't know where Aido is. If he's topped himself then he's a bloody coward for one and a fool for two. He's a cracker of a wife and three great wee kids." Mahood turned to look out across the factory.

"Do you think he's just thrown the toys out of the pram?" said Macpherson.

"Come here, look at this." Mahood moved back to his desk and half turned his monitor so the two detectives could see. Tapping in login details he then launched a selection of spreadsheets across two monitors.

"Mr Mahood, I don't know my arse from my elbow when it comes to those so you'll have to tell me what I'm supposed to be looking at." Macpherson had rifled a set of reading glasses from his inside pocket and peered at the screen. Taylor leaned in, suppressing a smile at the expression she had heard a hundred times before. The old dog wasn't daft but he couldn't stand the long way round or pretentious explanations, something Diane Pearson refrained from when delivering her forensic reports and which Professor Derek Thompson now watered down when he was wrist deep in a cadaver explaining the intricacies of cause of death.

Mahood smiled at the detective sergeant.

"Now you're a man after my own heart. I'll cut to the chase. We've two sets of transactions here, this one…" Mahood highlighted a column of cells, each colour coded and representing a financial transaction. "Shows payment made to a number of tender suppliers for R&D on a new inverter coil. Here, about three months ago, I told Aido to stop. After that, you can see at least another dozen transactions."

"He was co-director, and you admitted he's the more technical of the two of you. What's the issue?"

"The issue is I told him to stop because I had his theory independently reviewed and a paper presented on why it was too early to work. There were other developments needed, advancement in other parts of the design we aren't even close to engineering. You can't just drop a Ferrari engine in a bloody Nissan Micra, can you? And anyway, this inverter, it made no sense. There was a flaw with the design that I can't get my head around."

Macpherson harrumphed a nod at the analogy as Taylor looked down the column and mentally totted up. If Mahood was right, Quinn had been blowing the company's budget at a rate of knots for what would be no apparent return.

"I told him if we refocused on the plant expansion," Mahood held up a hand and counted off fingers. "One, more volume; more volume equals more sales and more profit. Two, investment in solar farms gives us a passive income. By the time the engineering problems had been worked around to suit the new invertors we would have already made the money back to explode out of the gate."

"When you asked him to stop pursuing this, do you think he continued? Somehow found an alternative means of funding?"

"He might have done but those two companies there, and a third, went to the wall over the last couple of months." Mahood shrugged. "As I said, what they proposed isn't the issue. It's that nobody is going to be able to use it."

Taylor considered the timetable and the actions of the man who from the germ of an idea and a deal of foresight had grown a shed project to something like Helios. Across the corridor outside Mahood's open door, Adrian Quinn's office lay dark. Nobody so far had said he was reckless, nor a gambler. If anything, Katherine Clark's revelation and his wife's corroboration that he put employee welfare before his family made the situation all the harder to fathom.

"There's no one else offering the same solution he might have tried?" said Taylor, noting down the company names.

"There's a reason all three of them are dead in the water."

"What's that other list?" said Macpherson. Mahood shook his head, a tick of frustration in the grind of his jaw.

"These are the company expense accounts."

He dragged the second spreadsheet over the top of the first on his main monitor screen.

"Who has access to that information?" said Taylor, skim reading the figures, pausing at some of the more eye-watering amounts.

"Me and Aido. My PA, Margaret East and Katherine Clark."

"So?" Macpherson thumbed his glasses back up his nose, the light of the monitor reflecting off the lenses.

"So unless I'm very much mistaken Bulgari, Louis Vuitton and a dozen treatments at a health clinic have fuck all to do with my business, and that's before all those cash withdrawals."

Taylor followed his finger as he highlighted the long list of spurious transactions.

"And it's not for client gifts or hospitality?" she said. Mahood scowled and shook his head.

"Did you talk to Adrian? Had he signed them off for Kath…" Macpherson's voice trailed off as Mahood continued to shake his head.

Taylor's phone began to ring as Mahood replied, she glanced down at the screen to see it was Erin Reilly.

"It wasn't Katherine," he said. "It was Aoife."

Chapter 13

A second cordon of red and white tape now fluttered in the breeze around the thirty-foot-wide depression at the bottom of the slope. In the centre, Diane Pearson and another member of her team carefully collected the contents of the bin liner, transferring each item and then the carrier bag itself into sealed plastic evidence bags.

"They confirmed blood on the branch and have it secured. Diane says she could be another half hour down here. What do you think?" said Walker.

Erin Reilly scanned the rutted undergrowth on which they stood, her eyes trailing back up the slope to where it was likely the bag had been flung, and then to her left where a significant stretch of vegetation showed signs of distress and damage to the thin, reedy branches of the trees and the supple ferns and bracken that nested at their feet. Working their way back up the hill, a section of the search team picked under loose leaves and slowly caressed the bank in a fingertip search to ensure no other items, either from what looked like Quinn's possessions or from anyone else had inadvertently been snagged.

"What do you think, Brian?" she said.

Brian Butler looked down at Flynn, who was prone on the forest floor happily chewing at her favourite tennis ball.

"Not a bother." He reached down to take the dog's ear and knead the velvety soft fur. "You ready again, girl?" Flynn dropped the ball and lay looking up with her deep brown eyes, her tongue flapping as she panted.

"This area here looks like someone trekked through," said Reilly, indicating the broken undergrowth. "Maybe whoever tossed the bag down saw it split and had to retrieve something, then, rather than scramble back up went through there. I can hear the river so there must be a towpath beyond this thicket?"

"Certainly looks like egress from this clearing." Brian Butler reached down to pluck up Flynn's toy, giving a nod of agreement.

"Go find, girl."

The dog let out an excited yelp and leapt to her feet, taking Butler's gestured command to follow the path leading out. Reilly called to the nearest searcher.

"Sarge, I need four of your lads to follow us, and then can I have the rest of the team conclude the search of the bank and then push out from this clearing on two vectors to intersect again with the running trail along the edge of Alpha?" She received a nod of understanding as the sergeant called out four names and directed them onto Reilly's heels. She strode briskly to catch up with Flynn, Butler and Walker.

"Did you see how happy she was to get that ball? Amazing isn't it," said Walker as she caught up, then as an afterthought. "Do you think we could get Doc one to bring him back down when he's off on one?" Reilly chuckled.

"If you hand Doc a tennis ball when he's up the high doh you may get to know a good surgeon."

Flynn was twenty feet ahead, steadily padding through a narrow track between the trees, her nose brushing from side to side and occasionally rooting through the longer grasses that edged what was opening up into a broader and more well-used track.

"She's got something, but she's sweeping," said Butler. "If there was transference or material taken from the clearing she'd go until she finds it or loses the scent. I'm watching for a snap of her head." He made a dog-head shape with his hand, touching two middle fingers to thumb, extending index and pinkie as ears and flicked his wrist. "If she catches a positive scent that will be the first indication."

Flynn continued to weave along the trampled path which rose up a short grassy bank before circling east toward the main trails. As the trees began to thin out and the sound of wild birds scattering in the trees sounded, Butler got the signal he was looking for. The dog's head cracked to the left and then dipped, her tail flattened, and she bounded off the track and into the undergrowth.

"Go on, after her," said Reilly with an excited lift in her voice as she ducked under a branch and heaved another bough of deadfall from her path.

The three moved as quickly and as carefully over the terrain as they could, the thumping steps of the four-man search squad following. She caught a shout from up ahead, pushing through vegetation to find Butler approaching his dog, cooing praise. Flynn wasn't paying any attention to the ball. She had flattened herself on the ground, laying across a patch of earth, scattered leaves and clumps of thick bracken.

"Hang on," Reilly raised a hand to the searchers. "The dog's got something. Usual protocol; work in from the outside, watch your step and keep your eyes peeled for secondary evidence."

Following her own advice and holding aside a branch for Walker, she stepped closer to Butler and the dog. The police constable's face had pinched, his expression one of concern.

"What's she got?" said Reilly.

"Nothing good," said Butler.

"Then what's she doing?" said Walker, coming to stand at Reilly's shoulder beside the handler and his dog.

"It the way she's laying. She'll only signal like that if she scents a cadaver."

"Shit," said Walker.

Reilly studied the dog; usually exuberant and ready to receive her reward she now instead lay prone, her chin to the ground between paws and her doleful brown eyes gazing up at Butler and the two detectives.

Reilly pulled out her phone.

Chapter 14

The splutter and rattle of petrol generators hummed in the distance as the cavalcade of police support vehicles taking over the Drumkeen Forest car park grew with each passing hour. Reilly had pulled the search team and, around the copse where Flynn had pinpointed the potential for a dead body, erected a cordon, the centre of which was now occupied by a four by four pop-up forensic tent and illuminated by half a dozen high-powered floodlights.

Inside, Diane Pearson and her initial team were supported by another crew from the forensic science lab at Seapark. Reilly herself was still clad in a Tyvek over suit from her initial walkthrough with the investigators before pulling back to let them take over the grim task of confirming Flynn's find.

"Did you not have any boots in the car, sarge?" said Chris Walker, standing a foot or so away from Reilly.

Macpherson glared up from looking down at his sodden shoes. Pressing the ball of his foot against a jutting rock sent the water seeping from the stitching of the well-worn leather.

"When you get to my age, we'll see how often you can be arsed to be bending down and changing your shoes, son," grumbled Macpherson, pulling the collar of his suit jacket up to ward off the whip of wind that had kicked up as dusk had dropped.

"I was a boy scout myself. Be prepared," said Walker, snapping off a salute and a grin.

"In my day we'd to go out to work from when we were ten years old. We'd no time for bloody dib dob or wiggle woggle. What's the craic with you, anyway? Is it fancy dress or what?"

Walker's grin slipped as he looked down at his attire. The DC had the look of the first day of term about him, although rather than a blazer and spit-shined shoes he wore a bright orange and blue GORE-TEX jacket, the hood now pulled up and drawstring tied in a neat bow under his chin, and a pair of matching waterproof over-trousers pulled over Barbour wellington boots.

"What's wrong with it?" said Walker, the dent in his pride peeking through in his question. Macpherson looked him up and down and gave a small smile.

"We'll not lose you in the dark, that's for sure."

"Leave him alone will you," said Erin Reilly, nudging the DS with an elbow. "I wish I'd thought of bringing something warmer."

"Yous are too bloody soft." Macpherson shook his head, straightening and jerking the lapels of his suit jacket, then, as a gust blew across the ridge, he batted away his fluttering tie. "I remember in my day—"

"Oh Christ, Chris. Where's the tennis ball?" said Reilly with a chuckle.

"Tennis ball?" Macpherson's face screwed up in confusion.

"I got it new," protested Walker. "I was thinking of doing a bit of trail walking, maybe seeing if I could volunteer a bit with the—"

"Aha!" Macpherson clapped his hands, his face cracked in mirth as he suddenly understood. "You're dolled up for your girlfriend, the bird lady."

"I am not…"

"You don't need to explain it to me, son," said Macpherson. "Fair play to you. I'm glad to see you finally putting yourself out there. Just maybe hold off asking her out until we've squared away the investigation." He gave the younger man a wink and Walker's face bloomed brighter than the patches on his coat as he turned away, grateful to see the tent's flap open and Diane Pearson peek out. She searched the commotion outside her forensic bubble, finally settling on a spot ten feet away from the trio where Taylor was in conversation with a uniformed inspector who had arrived to commandeer responsibility for the increased search team presence. Alongside them was one of Pearson's colleagues.

"Once the dog identified possible remains, we set the teams on a double back on the other deposition sites and concentrated on the routes from the car park to each. So far we've established a possible access route and two potential egress points from this clearing. I've stalled the search until first light and closed the park and established an outer cordon." Taylor nodded as the inspector concluded the update.

"What about people already on site?"

"I've officers in the car park making enquiries of anyone returning to their vehicle and two cyclists doing a route of the trails to round up anybody still here. There's a lot of ground to cover and it's as leaky as a sieve."

Taylor knew the task was unenviable. The forest park covered an extensive area and could not only be accessed from the main entrance but a host of other points around the perimeter from residential gardens and towpath walks along from the Lagan Meadow and Shaw's Bridge to other conservation and picnic spots like the one sited at the Lockkeeper's Cottage.

"We've only released the details to the press this morning. Do your best to maintain the integrity of the sites. If this is bad news, I'd rather get a chance to tell Aoife Quinn to her face before there are pictures of a burial site on the tabloid websites."

The inspector nodded his understanding but also gave a shrug. Taylor returned the gesture. She knew he would try to, and she wouldn't hang him if somebody did sneak through and out the discovery before the press team could do it.

"Mal?" Taylor gave Pearson's deputy a jerk of her chin.

"We've confirmed the presence of blood on a branch collected near the entrance to the trails and the clothing collected from site two matches the description you supplied of Adrian Quinn's gear. There was a matching Under Armour soft-shell jacket in the car. The branch, the clothing and the bag that contained them have been sent back to Seapark for further tests."

"Smashing. What about in there?" said Taylor, turning to see Pearson duck under the cordon, and drop her mask and hood.

"Hiya," said Pearson in greeting, reaching down to her kitbag to remove a bottle of diet cola. It opened with a long hiss, and she took a swig.

"Di, what's the craic? Anything for me inside?" said Taylor.

Pearson slowly recapped the cola and shook out her ash blonde hair into the breeze.

"Initial search by K9 identified possible remains. I'd say, by what I've seen so far, what we're looking at in the tent is potentially a deposition site. Six by six-foot-square of recently disturbed earth with a rudimentary attempt to disguise the excavation after the fact with deadfall and uprooted flora and fauna. Could be a forensic goldmine for fibres, hair, possibly DNA once we can properly access the burial, but first things first, we're about to start taking off the first layer of soil."

"Anything else we can do?" said Taylor. Pearson shook her head.

"For the sake of three wee kiddies, cross your fingers it's not what we're all thinking." Pearson gave a resigned half shake of her head. "You ready, Mal?"

The deputy forensic officer gave an assured nod and ducked under the tape, holding it up for his boss, who followed, raising her hood and re-securing her mask.

"Not good news then?" said Macpherson as Taylor approached her team.

"Di says it's odds on they'll find a body."

"Jesus," mumbled Macpherson, suddenly feeling the evening chill and wrapping his arms around his chest.

"Guv." Erin Reilly appeared from behind the two, absent the Tyvek over suit and wearing a police baseball cap. A scarf wrapped around her neck was tucked into an oversized police fleece jacket. She offered an identical garment to Macpherson.

"Had a few going spare," she said, nodding back to the car park. Macpherson looked at her outstretched hand, Reilly briefly thinking he might refuse, until he nodded gratefully and shrugged his arms into the fleece and pulled the zipper right up to his chin.

Taylor looked down at the forensic tent. Already illuminated from within by portable battery lights, the brighter flare of a camera flash lit the sides. Pearson, she knew, would document every skim of soil that was scraped from the surface and her eye for detail and complete dedication to her art would sift the material for any singular piece of matter that in some way did not belong until she revealed the body.

The trees swayed in the gathering breeze and the callous caws of roosting rooks seemed to mock the DI as she cast her eyes in thought up to the bony branches and considered where the day had brought them. Her overriding thoughts lingered on how whatever was about to be revealed may close the initial phase of the case and kick it into a much higher gear; while one question would sadly be answered it left a list of others and while separate, each felt as tangled with the next as the overcooked spaghetti in one of Macpherson's Bolognese dishes.

Another flash lit the fabric of the tent and she plotted a mental map of the forest; from Quinn's car to the alleged altercation with Kilburn, the dump of clothing, and here, a quarter mile further to what might be a final resting place. Whatever was going on with his business life in Helios, was it enough to end a life? Mahood was certainly a force of nature. But a murderer? And as complex as the relationship was between the two men, Quinn's personal ties to Katherine Clark, the veiled undercurrent of marital disharmony and financial irregularity added an unwelcome and intangible layer of suspicion on the women.

Taylor pondered the possibility of any one of those two quietly dispatching Quinn and manhandling him to this remote spot unseen with scepticism. But when she considered Jackie Mahood or indeed Raymie Kilburn, there was not so much doubt. Not unless there was a combination of factors and actors. She started as the door flaps to the tent opened and Diane Pearson stepped out.

Her thoughts along with the muted conversation on the outside of the tape faded to absolute silence as the senior forensic investigator approached. Pearson shook her head sadly.

"It's a grave alright," she said.

"Quinn?" said Taylor, the cordon tape fluttering against her thighs.

Pearson shook her head again.

"No. Somebody's buried a dozen dead puppies."

Chapter 15

"You're quiet this morning? You didn't hit the Maharaja on the way home last night, did you?"

Macpherson gave a weary smile and a small shake of his head, lowering the driver's window to allow in a stream of cool, refreshing air as he turned the Volvo into Bladon Manor.

"Didn't sleep too well."

Taylor looked across at her friend and surrogate father figure. The man who had practically raised her following the death of her parents, and guided her through her formative years as a student and police officer, had three moods. A grim dourness he reserved for his work, a deep loving warmth for the family he embraced in his huge bear hugs and a melancholy that appeared from time to time. The first she knew was an act, for the man's heart was as big as his hands and while he was direct and sometimes abrupt he only had an interest in developing his colleagues and subordinates to be the best investigators they could be, and to be embraced by the second was to know the love and loyalty of a man who would unquestioningly move heaven and earth for a friend. The third was more complex and one that touched most of her colleagues at some point; it could at times roll in and disperse as quickly as a summer storm, or it could build slowly and darken the edges of the mind like angry black clouds settling upon the craggy peak of the Cavehill.

It wasn't entirely unexpected that spending hours, days, weeks and months engaged in a profession that saw them deal with the worst humanity could offer, seeing firsthand the personal toll it took on victims, their families and wider communities would eventually tip the scales and produce either an outburst of emotion as thoughts and feelings were processed or a closing down as the cork was wedged in further to bottle up those personal opinions that might threaten impartiality and duty.

Taylor laid her hand on his forearm as he changed down a gear, approaching the Quinn household, knowing that while Macpherson held no aversion to man's inhumanity to man, when those callous and vindictive crimes crossed species to affect innocent and defenceless animals he struggled to maintain his professional equilibrium.

"Couldn't get the thought of them wee dogs out of my head," he said glancing at her, then back out the windscreen. "We see some shite day-to-day but every now and again there's one wee thing just gets under your skin."

"I know." Taylor gave him an empathetic smile.

"God love them," said Macpherson. His jaw pulsed as he gritted his teeth and pulled up outside the house.

God love them indeed, thought Taylor, thinking not only of the tiny sleek bodies of the Staffordshire bull terrier pups but also the three Quinn children and what they might soon be going through.

❖❖❖

"I need to get this one to school," said Aoife Quinn. She had one hand on the door and in the other held the hand of her daughter, Sophie. The little girl peered round from behind her mother to look up at the two detectives. Somewhere deeper in the house a plaintive wail rose from another sibling to be echoed a moment later by the other.

"It won't take long."

"Has something happened?"

"Might be better if we came inside," said Macpherson, and whether it was due to his look or the hangover of melancholy in his tone, Quinn eased the door aside and ushered them in.

"Sophie, go and get your bag and break," said Quinn. The little girl complied without question and danced off into the kitchen. Quinn opened a panelled door and let the two officers enter a bright day room before following.

The room was carpeted in a thick fawn wool blend, the vacuum marks still apparent on the surface, and one wall was papered in gold floral wallpaper, the colour adding to the warm ambience of the room. A white marbled fireplace with a brass insert and two, red, three-seater sofas were illuminated by a large bay window and a dozen downlighters set in a corniced bulkhead and an elegant central ceiling light.

"What's happened?" said Quinn, partially closing the door but not shutting it.

"We've discovered some of Adrian's clothing near where his car was parked."

"I don't understand? What do you mean by some of his clothing, like his jacket or something?"

Taylor shared a brief look with her DS.

"Take a seat, Mrs Quinn."

"No. Tell me what you mean."

"We found your husband's running gear discarded in woodland near the trail on which he was last seen."

"But how? I… I'm sorry, you're not making any sense."

"No, I'm sure we're not," agreed Taylor. "Clothing items matching the descriptions you supplied to us were found in a bin bag amongst the undergrowth. We've recovered them for analysis."

Quinn finally sat, although Taylor wondered how much of

it was a conscious decision and how much was her legs going out from under her.

"Was there any sign of…" Quinn cut herself off and once again Taylor knew she was avoiding tempting fate.

"No, our search led to several other areas but so far no sign of your husband."

"Is that all you've come to tell me?" A hint of anguished aggression sprang up in Quinn's voice, at once elated they weren't there with bad news but tempered by the fact there was no further progress.

"Actually we spent some time at Helios last night and have a few questions you might be able to help us with."

"About Helios? There'd be better-placed people to help you with that, Inspector."

"It's about your husband's expense account."

"And?"

"And there's a list of transactions we need some clarity on."

Quinn narrowed her eyes. She had propped an elbow on the arm of the chair and angled her closed knees away from the two officers who now sat ninety degrees to her left on a matching sofa.

"What kind of transactions?"

Macpherson removed the printed list of expenses Mahood had furnished them with the evening before.

"Do you have access to your husband's company credit card?"

"No."

"Mrs Quinn, I'm not interested in whether you've broken Helios policy or not by using company credit for personal purchases. I just want to know what the cash withdrawals were for?"

"What are you talking about?"

Macpherson brandished the list, stood and took a step

towards her, handing it over.

"Mr Mahood singled these out as transactions outside the scope of normal expenditure. You'll see reading down. Somebody went on quite the spree. Jewellery, high-end fashion outlets—"

"This wasn't me…"

"Mrs Quinn, Jackie Mahood spotted this a while ago but chose to keep an eye on it rather than raise it as an issue with your husband. He suggests his enquires with the stores identified you as the client in the transactions."

"Right, okay, so what if I bought a few things? It was my husband's company." Quinn seemed non-plussed now she had been rumbled, thought Taylor, maybe even a little hostile, as though this was the first opportunity she'd had to vent her frustrations. Perhaps she had supposed she would be caught in the act by her husband; an excuse for confrontation over money and matrimonial obligations.

"As I said, Mrs Quinn, I don't care about shoes and handbags. I'm more concerned over the thousands of pounds of cash withdrawals."

"That wasn't me."

"Mrs Quinn, we can request ATM and bank CCTV. Our investigations are leaning towards your husband being in financial difficulty, which was exacerbated as his access to regular company credit was under scrutiny. Did he have you access this cash for a reason? Did he tell you he needed it to further research or pay suppliers? Maybe even pay off a loan shark."

"A loan shark?"

"It's an avenue we are considering."

Quinn shook her head vehemently. "No."

"Mrs Quinn, it might help us uncover what's happened to Adrian if we understand to what extent he was in trouble?"

"I'm telling you it wasn't me." Quinn had scanned the list

and pointed triumphantly at a line item. She thrust the list back at Macpherson, storming out to return a second later. In her hand, she brandished a hospital appointment card.

"There you go. Take that away and check. I was at hospital with the twins when I was supposed to be lifting five grand from the bank." She waved the appointment card and when neither detective reached for it she put it on the sofa between them. "Go on. Go and check."

"Mrs Quinn…" said Taylor.

Aoife Quinn opened the day room door wide.

"I want you to go. I need to take my daughter to school."

Chapter 16

"Thanks, Carrie, you're a lifesaver." Macpherson accepted the two paracetamol and cup of black coffee from Carrie Cook.

The team were sitting around the same table in briefing room 4.12 as they had been the previous day, although this time they had significantly more information but also an equal number of questions that needed answers.

"You look like you need a day off," said Cook, sitting opposite.

"Bad night that's all." Macpherson averted his eyes, avoiding any further engagement in conversation as to why he wasn't his usual gruff self, and Walker for once seemed to read the tension and refrained from making any digs with his sparring partner.

The monitor at the head of the table displayed a rifle green background and the Police Service of Northern Ireland crest.

Taylor waited until her DS had necked the pills and taken a swig of the coffee, accepting his stiff nod as his signal he was ready to get on with proceedings. Cook had rigged up the long HDMI cable and connected the screen to her laptop and was busy logging in.

Erin Reilly had her own laptop in front of her and was busy organising the various emails and updates that had come in overnight from the forensic science laboratory at Seapark while Walker pondered the ordinance survey map that was laid out, carefully folded to show the southeast of the city and the area and roadways around the Drumkeen Estate and forest park.

There was a knock on the door which opened to admit Detective Chief Inspector Gillian Reed. She waved them to ease and took up a position at the head of the table to Taylor's left.

"Morning, I won't keep you from the coal face but I've to appraise the chief super in five, and the press office has been in contact with queries from a few of the local print and TV outlets regarding our operation at Drumkeen Forest Park. I've seen from the initial reports that we had mixed results, so, have we had any developments overnight from the items recovered?"

Gillian Reed exuded a calm and measured demeanour, and while those colleagues and crooks who were not in the know often mistook her for a bean counter or the duty brief, the DCI was a seasoned detective, forged in the fires of division and sectarian conflict, albeit in designer heels and looking like she had stepped out of a shop window.

"It's a bit early, ma'am. The items recovered matched those described as belonging to Adrian Quinn but forensics are yet to return any confirmation of positive trace on them or the log recovered." Taylor glanced at Reilly as she spoke, receiving a nod of confirmation.

"And the deposition site?"

"Negative. No traces of Quinn."

"That's something I suppose," said Reed, using a pair of horn-rimmed spectacles to better review the information Carrie Cook had launched onto the monitor.

"The site contained the bodies of twelve young staffies." Taylor took a quick look at Macpherson who had half turned in his chair and by the bulge in his jaw was gritting his teeth. "We know there is an element within the estate who use the forest for dog fighting and badger baiting, so I expect these were just unwanted pups. Callous but…" Taylor shrugged.

"I take it we ticked all the boxes, Veronica?"

Taylor nodded, knowing the DCI hadn't come up the Lagan in a bubble.

"Forensics removed the animals and carried out an extensive dig and investigation to ensure they weren't decoys for other remains."

Taylor raised a finger to Cook, who pulled up the site photos of Pearson's excavation. The soil had been carefully removed, and each layer photographed; an occasional glare of Tyvek over suit or a gloved hand was caught in the camera's flash as the slideshow detailed the dig to expose the dogs and then a deeper dig to ensure nothing was buried underneath, the tactic of a decoy often used by organised criminal gangs as a means of subterfuge in the disposal of something else.

"Okay, anything else at the minute?"

"We've established Quinn hasn't used his mobile phone since the morning of his disappearance, Chris?"

"That's right, Mr Quinn made two calls on the morning before he went missing. One to the switchboard at Helios and a second to an unregistered mobile. On that, we've no further hits, no calls, no triggers on masts or GPS. It's likely it ran out of battery or was turned off," said Walker.

"And the car?"

"Other than superficial damage, forensically clean aside from Quinn, his wife and his daughter. We're checking the onboard GPS."

Reed nodded and, satisfied for the moment, stood.

"What's the direction this morning?"

"We're about to review the Quinns' financial position to

see if it may be relevant to his disappearance and some follow-up on Helios."

"Let me know if Seapark returns anything." Taylor nodded, the sentence ambiguous but the meaning behind implicit. Was there blood on the clothes and is this a murder investigation.

"Ma'am."

Reed exited, closing the door behind her. Taylor waited a beat.

"Erin, keep one eye on those reports from Diane. Give us the nod when they land. Carrie, do you want to kick off?"

"All set, so, I followed up on your requests. First off, the Quinns' nuisance calls. We've a few." Cook dragged and dropped a spreadsheet of call histories and expanded the window for ease of view.

"Two specifically; this one ending in seven, one, zero by far the more persistent and the other four, four, eight coming at more irregular intervals."

"Did you manage to identify which called when we were there?" said Macpherson.

"I did, and narrowing down to those specifics it was seven, one, zero and I've a match. Katherine Clark."

"The PA?"

Cook nodded. Taylor considered what it meant. Clark and Aoife were known to each other, and although the relationship was likely strained because of Quinn's infidelity, why did Clark not speak, even to ask if there was any news. She came to a conclusion at the same time as Macpherson.

"Aoife Quinn knew who was calling and didn't engage."

Taylor nodded.

"Passive-aggressive punishment? My husband might be missing, but it's nothing to do with you?" suggested Cook.

"Maybe, was there a history prior to…" Cook was nodding as Taylor drifted off.

"Absolutely. Loads of calls over the last weeks and months. A few lasted several seconds, some up to half an hour."

"Which suggests Quinn himself was taking those," said Taylor. "Okay, we'll have another word with Clark. What about the other number?"

"Similar pattern. Numerous calls over the last few months. No discernible pattern and no call time to suggest conversation, although there's one significant finding."

"It's the same number that Quinn called the day of his disappearance," said Walker.

"We've nothing else?" said Taylor

"Not a thing." Both Cook and Walker shook their heads.

"Okay, Carrie, prioritise this number and pass it on to intel. If it pings or comes up against anything else, we need to know."

"Guv."

"How did the finances look?" Cook closed the call histories and brought up the financial records.

"There are a few different accounts, personal banking, savings and credit. Payment history shows he's avoided defaults as far back as recorded. You'll see the savings accounts which were riding high eighteen months ago have taken a battering when the funds were transferred into these two cash accounts. There's also a hefty re-mortgage."

The team followed Cook's cursor as she highlighted the rows and columns of transactions.

"That puts him well over his credit utilisation, which places him now in the risk bracket for most lenders. Card payments have run up over the same period and there's been quite a few cash advances. The regular end of month clearance has also changed to minimum payment."

"His company card needed stitches too, the battering it was getting." Macpherson pointed at the screen. "Are those ATM withdrawals?"

"Yes. Sometimes two or three a day."

"Did you get through the report from Jackie Mahood?" said Taylor. Cook nodded.

"Not all of it, but most of the cash withdrawals correspond with these personal withdrawals."

"Like he was pulling out cash on both cards at the same time?" said Walker.

Cook nodded again. "We're looking at a few cards linked to the company. I confirmed his wife's hospital appointment which corroborates Aoife Quinn didn't make a cash withdrawal, at least in that one instance. We're still open to her being able to access one of the cards for other spend though."

"And those transactions?"

"Mainly high-end boutiques and jewellers. Dropped a few grand on clothing in Victoria Square and at a diamond merchant off Ann Street, ah…" Cook skimmed a few pages of the itemised transactions and her follow-ups. "A few of the shop owners knew Quinn by name, several confirmed a customer matching her description. Callan's of Castle Lane confirmed a transaction of three grand for a twenty-four-carat white gold chain with a curled-u pendant? No idea what that means."

"She was fairly getting payback for his trip behind the bike sheds with Clark," said Macpherson. He had leaned forward and was scanning each of the eye-watering amounts on the list. Walker smirked as Reilly tapped on the keys of her laptop. Taylor was glad to see Macpherson's morose mood had been lifted with the advent of more work.

"It's a bird," said Reilly, spinning her laptop around.

"Ah, a curlew?" said Walker, nodding appreciatively at the website listing for the chain and pendant. "You can tell by the bill."

"Three grand is some bill, David Attenborough,"

murmured Macpherson, toying with the rim of his plastic coffee cup.

"The bill." Walker tapped the screen. "They're one of Europe's largest wading birds. Amazing, isn't it? They spend the winter along the coast, on the mudflats and estuaries before moving inland to breed. Places like Lagan Meadows or the marshes and arable fields, you know, like the ones bordering Drumkeen Forest Park." Walker had a grin from ear to ear as he regaled the room with his knowledge.

"Tell you what, your girlfriend's going to be beside herself if you keep up that talk," said Macpherson, brightening. Walker's face turned sombre.

"They're on the red list, a high risk of extinction." He shook his head sadly.

"Bit of advice, son, you were doing well up to extinction. Death talk's a passion killer."

As Walker rolled his eyes, the rest of the team gave a relaxed chuckle. Taylor seeing the mirth returned to Macpherson's eyes gave him a nod which he reciprocated. An unspoken gesture that he was fine.

"Pay him no heed, Chris," said Taylor. "We all need a hobby and there's worse you could be doing, like hustling half the Law Society at poker."

Macpherson shook his head, an expression of innocence on his face.

"For supposedly intelligent professionals, I can't for the life of me work out how they don't know when to fold."

It was Cook who drew the conversation back to the task at hand.

"Speaking of extinction, based on what I can see here, Quinn was heading towards having his own lights put out if he continued at this level of spending."

"Which brings us to his rescue plan, the ill-fated expansion deal," said Taylor.

"And coincidently breeding grounds." Cook killed the financial spreadsheets and drew up a collection of Google maps and images of farmland. "These are the three sites acquired for the expansion project. Each had achieved planning status for a PV installation over three acres per location. The concern raised by the environmental groups is that these areas border protected habitat for migratory birds and the impact of construction would be detrimental to that habitat and the wildlife's survival."

"Shocking." Walker shook his head. Cook flicked up another screen.

"This is the contentious one Katherine Clark highlighted. It was initially for sale with approved planning permission for two hundred homes. It looks like Helios made a bid for that and also managed to acquire the area behind it which was dead ground and council owned. The paperwork designates it as the location for a new Helios production facility, although there's a question mark over this as Helios also have an acquisition a few miles away for that."

Taylor looked at the shaded plan view of an area that cut across from the southern end of the Annadale Embankment, hemmed in on one side by the river and the other by the A24, and nestled near Drumkeen Park Golf club and the edge of the forest.

"Any idea why Adrian Quinn would veto it?" she said.

"You mentioned substrate, but it passed all the regulatory controls and was on sale for residential build. Bar objections similar to the ones Helios are battling, nothing leaps out."

"Clark said he wanted an area with enough land around to create a parkland," said Macpherson. "An olive branch to the other side?"

"And given that location, he couldn't do that." Taylor nodded.

"Why is Mahood so adamant to get his hands on it?" said

Reilly.

"Probably only one reason. He knows if he owns that land, the price is going in one direction. Look what's around him, everything is protected and no one can ever build on it. With the rate that building expansion is moving towards the outskirts, in a few years, he could offload that site for a fortune." Taylor could see now why Mahood was eager to seal the deal for the land but not why Quinn didn't buy into what seemed like a shrewd deal. As she sought an angle, there was a knock on the door and Leigh-Anne Arnold peeked in.

"Ma'am?"

"Leigh-Anne?"

"I thought you'd want to see this." Arnold handed over her mobile.

A Facebook live stream was underway and showing an altercation between a group of individuals and an angry mob. The camerawork was poor and the images jumpy, but she still identified the logo and the galvanised fence around Helios. The crowd seemed to be outside and pressed up against the gates.

"Is this another protest?"

Arnold shook her head.

"That's the workforce. They're saying on here Helios has shut up shop. For good."

Chapter 17

"....at the renewable technology company's headquarters in south Belfast. It's reported Helios has ceased all production, with one worker at the factory which produces photovoltaic panels telling this programme the news was delivered this morning out of the blue by a factory manager. This devastating blow for the company and the workforce comes amid the ongoing search for their founder and company director, Adrian Quinn, who was last seen..."

Macpherson pulled the Volvo to a stop a hundred yards from the gate as there was no way to get any closer. The narrow road was choked with Helios staff, some still in their protective coveralls or hi-vis vests, milling about on the road in front of the closed iron gates.

A police patrol car had managed to negotiate the human barrier and was now parked across the entrance, two constables just about holding back the tide of discontent and shock that minute by minute was building through the masses.

"What's the craic?" Macpherson jerked his head toward the factory, where a group of women stood on the periphery of the crowd, marked out as office administration by their navy attire and Helios branded pale blue blouses.

"Told us they had to close..."

"Aye, first thing." A second woman nodded, dragging on a cigarette. She blew a cloud of smoke into the air. "Gathered everybody up and said with Mr Quinn missing and losses over the past year they couldn't sustain the business."

"Load of shite…" muttered a third.

"Who delivered the news?" said Taylor.

"Seawright."

"Where's Mr Mahood?"

"Didn't see him, the yellow bastard, but his car's in there."

"Thanks."

"Can they do this?"

"Is this not against our worker's rights?"

"My personal stuff's still in there…"

Taylor and Macpherson moved toward the gate. Neither had an answer to the questions that erupted behind them.

The antagonism and fervent anger in the crowd grew as they approached the gate and with the absence of company bosses to take the flack, it was beginning to fall on the two constables as the comments continued.

"Joke. It's a frigging joke…"

"We're the ones in the right here…"

"What are you protecting them thieves for? What about my pension?"

"Ma'am, sarge." One of the constables gave a nod as the two detectives eased through the bodies, Taylor brandishing her warrant card and Macpherson with an expression that would sour milk when any of the protesting employees made to challenge their progress.

"What happened?"

"Got a call to attend when the printing unit across the road reported that this was kicking off."

"Anything serious?"

The constable turned down his mouth. "Not really, catcalling and a bit of grandstanding by shop steward types."

The constable glanced over her shoulder at what was slowly descending into a mob, a few rabble rousers now taking up chants against Helios, Jackie Mahood, and the police protection. He gave Taylor a half shake of the head, which she returned in understanding, the thin blue line once again tasked with keeping apart the disaffected masses from the object of their discontent. It was a shared experience they had both endured and which thankfully at the moment didn't involve petrol bombs and slabs of broken up pavement.

"Can you let us in?"

"Aye, come on." He gave a stern look at the front lines as he pulled up the locking bolt and then slid the gate latch, granting eighteen inches of space to squeeze through before he slammed the locks home again behind them.

The noise seemed weirdly louder this side of the fence, thought Taylor, unable to strike the images of an old black-and-white Hammer horror movie from her mind, the looming shadow of Helios Sustainable cast as the bastion of the beast and all that was missing from the mob outside was their torch and pitchforks.

"Is Mr Seawright about?" said Taylor

There was one young girl still at reception and their arrival had caught her unawares. The switchboard under her gaze was lit up like the city on the eleventh night, and the piles of filing and paperwork around her ankles were stacked as precariously as the bonfires themselves.

"How did you get past—"

"We're with the police." Taylor saw a fleeting expression cross her face and saw a family resemblance. "Is he your daddy?"

The girl nodded.

"We know the way, pet," said Macpherson, giving her a sympathetic smile. There was a fear on her face, one that said the affection of her peers was now very much absent.

As they ascended the stairs, Taylor noted the lights in Adrian Quinn's office were on but no one was in the room. A few filing cabinets had drawers open as did his desk and it was the same for Mahood's, except his office looked much less ransacked than the former. Entering Seawright's they found him also absent, although as they returned to the head of the stairs his voice could be heard from a room at the end of the landing.

"Mr Seawright?"

"Hello? Oh…"

"I'd normally ask if it was a bad time but I'd say that's a given."

Richard Seawright looked frayed to the edges. He was sat in the centre of a long conference table with a spider phone pulled towards him and a legal pad filled with scribbles under his hands.

"You can't imagine."

"What's going on?" said Macpherson, easing around to the left and leaning against the wall under the company name which was fixed in brushed steel letters.

"We're handing over to the administrators and I'm trying to collate all the pertinent records associated with the last financial quarter and collate a list of debtors and creditors."

"Is the boss about?" said Taylor, nodding out the window behind Seawright to the large green Discovery.

"Jackie?" Seawright's voice broke, and he gave a nervous cough.

"Unless Adrian Quinn's turned up?" said Macpherson.

"I don't think that's going to happen?"

"Is that right? You know a bit more than us then, so you do." The DS pushed off the wall to walk over to the window.

"I just mean… Jackie's not here, alright."

"So is that scotch mist down there?" said Macpherson, pulling apart the slats of the blinds. The movement sent a roar of noise up from the crowd at the gate.

"His car? His car's here but he's not." Seawright was beginning to stammer.

"Mr Seawright, what happened? What's driven this since our last conversation" Taylor drew out a chair and sat; Seawright closed his eyes and rubbed the bridge of his nose.

"I took a call from Jackie this morning. He said he had no joy with securing reinvestment and that the finances were in worse shape than he had thought. He didn't give any specifics, but he left no room for doubt we weren't going to recover and he issued the directive to halt production with immediate effect and inform the staff we were to close."

"He's not a one-man band, fella. He can't do that without Adrian Quinn approving." Macpherson had taken a perch on the edge of the table.

"That's what I said." Seawright pulled a finger around the collar of his shirt. "He told me he had executive power as Adrian wasn't coming back."

"He said that?" Macpherson's face darkened as he shared a look with Taylor.

"Or words to that effect."

"Had he been speaking to Adrian?" said Taylor, trying to see beyond Seawright's flustered anxiety.

"Not as far as I'm aware. He made a more general comment about the news of your search in Drumkeen Forest finding something. A… a… a body."

Taylor tapped her fingernail against her front teeth.

"While I can't divulge anything regarding what was found last night, Mr Seawright, I can tell you this remains a missing person's investigation."

"So Adrian's alive?" For the first time since they had walked into the room, Richard Seawright's tone was imbued with a sliver of optimism.

For the sake of his three little kiddies, I hope so, thought

Taylor but as she looked around the room at the scattered lists of debts and listened to the angry calls outside she couldn't help but wonder that if Quinn was to be found alive, aside from the physical embrace of his family just what exactly would be left to return to.

Chapter 18

"Just a second." There was a scrape of keys across wood and then a rattle as the contents of the keyring jangled against the door lock. "Oh… it's yourselves. Is something wrong?"

Laura Roberts recovered her shock quickly enough and presented Reilly and then Chris Walker with one of her beaming smiles.

"We're sorry to drop in on you at home, Miss Roberts," said Reilly, returning the smile. "We tried at the forest park but it was shut up."

"There didn't seem much point opening up; your colleagues are still there and the paths are closed to the public. I've some work I can be getting on with from here." Roberts looked relaxed, her hair was loose, and she was barefoot, wearing a pair of skinny blue jeans and a cream cowl necked tee shirt under a cardigan in the same shade. She toyed with a chain around her neck, waiting with patience tinged with a little curiosity for the police officers to explain their trip to her home.

"We're sorry about that, it's an inconvenience, I'm sure. Could we come in?" said Reilly.

Roberts hesitated for a fraction of a second and then took a step back.

"Sure, but please ignore the mess." She skipped up the

hallway ahead of them, taking a right turn into the lounge.

The trip out to Roberts' house had taken only half an hour or so and with the sun shining it had made for a pleasant journey, heading east across the Queen Elizabeth Bridge and quickly leaving behind the city and the suburbs as they headed for the commuter town of Newtownards and then skirting around the A20, under the watchful eye of Scrabo tower they continued into the countryside proper, hugging the peninsula with emerald green fields on one side and the shimmering waters of Strangford Lough on the other.

Reilly had expected Roberts' statement to be the polite and modest aside people generally made when accepting unexpected visitors into their home but as she entered the lounge, to her surprise she found that her hesitation was warranted and likely stemmed from embarrassment.

The homeowner pulled aside a set of drapes to let in sunlight, offering a view of the lough at the end of her garden, "Grab a seat, I'll be two seconds," she said, passing Reilly to stoop and gather up an ashtray in one hand and a wine bottle and glasses with the other. Walker raised an eyebrow as he moved to take an armchair. Roberts had opened a window, but the breeze hadn't killed the smell of marijuana.

"Drink?" she called from the kitchen. Reilly noted a tightness in her voice and pictured the woman looking at her reflection and swearing inwardly to herself at the awkwardness of the situation.

"We're grand, thanks," said Reilly. "And sorry, I promise we won't take up much of your time." She hoped her tone gave some comfort that they weren't about to haul her in for possession.

The coffee table displayed some official-looking paperwork and a collection of gold foil chocolate wrappers, which Roberts swept up as she returned to the room. She balled the wrappers and tossed them atop the spent ashes of an open fire and set the other documents on top of a bookcase to the right of the chair which Walker had chosen. He blushed, averting his eyes as her top rode up, revealing a flat midriff and the lacy trim of her underwear. Roberts gave a small smile as she turned, adjusting her clothes and her necklace.

"I heard on the news there was some kind of discovery, I hope...."

"It's still a missing person's case," said Reilly. Roberts nodded, acknowledging the pair weren't about to reveal too much more.

"So, you need some help?" she said.

Reilly removed a selection of photographs from the document wallet she carried.

"Could you have a look at these? The CCTV we initially viewed is helpful, but it doesn't give us much detail. We're trying to eliminate some people and vehicles from the enquiry." The DC brushed her blonde fringe from her eyes as she first laid out a catalogue picture of a dark blue Ford Everest.

"Is this the model of vehicle you saw boxing-in the BMW?"

Roberts leaned forward, studying the picture. She absentmindedly tapped her silver chain off her chin as she did.

"Could be?"

"But you're not sure?

"Not a car buff I'm afraid," said Roberts, sitting back.

"That's okay," said Reilly as she removed a half dozen headshots. Among them were Adrian Quinn, Jackie Mahood and Raymond Kilburn.

"What about any of these men?"

Roberts' finger went straight to Quinn. "That's the man who drove the BMW."

"Anyone else? Specifically, the man you saw arguing with

him?"

Roberts pored over the remaining pictures, her eyes drifting to Adrian Quinn now sitting apart. There was silence as she concentrated, the lough-side house creaking with the sort of noises associated with a smallholding exposed to the coast and the elements. Above, the floorboards groaned as though someone had shifted in bed or the central heating had come on and was expanding the old joists. Roberts finally broke the silence.

"Have you any idea where he is?" Reilly shook her head.

"That's why whatever help you can give us could be vital."

Roberts nodded slowly, her gaze drifting back from Quinn to the line-up. She reached out a finger, heading for Jackie Mahood until at the last second she slid out the photo of Raymond Kilburn.

"This one."

"Sure?"

"Pretty sure."

Reilly glanced up at Walker, who was watching Roberts with rapt attention.

Chapter 19

Taylor and Macpherson had just exited the lift and were returning to the blue baize cubicles of CID when a familiar voice broke their stride.

"Inspector?"

"Chief Superintendent."

William Law looked like a man on a mission; his strides marked time along the hallway with a clipped beat, his boots were shined to parade perfection and the dress uniform he wore was unblemished with not so much as a blade-sharp seam out of place or an epaulette badge that wasn't exquisite in alignment or radiance. He carried his cap in his left hand, the peak gleaming like a curved black mirror.

"Helios and this Quinn business."

"Yes, sir?"

"I've had Charlotte Quigley on demanding an answer as to why nearly two hundred of her constituents have been made unemployed in the blink of an eye." He stopped at attention two feet from the two officers, Taylor easing a step between the two men, eager to avoid either Macpherson dropping an inappropriate comment or his appearance drawing any ire from their rigorous superior.

"Down Under has some cheek getting on the phone when she couldn't be arsed standing up for the freeze on our pay," huffed Macpherson, following up with a tut and a shake of the head. Law's face bled puce from his starched collar to his forehead, his eyebrows dancing like angry caterpillars.

"Sergeant, should you need reminding, Ms Quigley is an elected representative in an area where fifty per cent of the community still don't wholly trust us and the other half hold us in contempt. I don't think throwing her weight behind a campaign to ensure you can afford to go to Portugal instead of Portstewart on your holidays, aids the delicate balance of diplomacy."

"Maybe there wouldn't be so much contempt if she wasn't so keen on swapping handshakes and blank cheques with Gordon Beattie... sir."

"Chief Superintendent." Taylor jumped in, desperate to divert the conversation away from the notorious gangland figure turned business magnate and the memories and dark period of personal history he represented.

"We've just come from Helios. The firm is being handed to the administrators. Jackie Mahood gave instructions to his plant manager to break the news this morning. They've suffered significant financial impacts over the last quarter and the business, according to him, is no longer viable."

"They were winning awards and on the cover of the Business Eye not two months ago, where's the money and where is Adrian bloody Quinn?"

"We're just on our way to review where we are on that with DC Cook, sir, and we're waiting on forensic results from Seapark following last night's search. As soon as they're in, I'll appraise the DCI."

"See that you do, and see if you can make it sooner rather than later, Inspector."

Macpherson managed to refrain from saying anything else as Law about-turned and marched back the way he had come.

❖❖❖

"…more interested in the larger transactions than the smaller quantities we are thinking link to Aoife Quinn on a spending spree."

Cook had once again rigged up the monitor in 4.12 and was giving Taylor and Macpherson an overview of the expense report supplied by Mahood and information she was able to glean from Companies House on the business and its official financial reporting.

"What have you highlighted those for?" Taylor pointed out a set of yellow cells.

"Those fifteen transactions do match with Aoife Quinn. They are withdrawals from forecourt ATMs at two filling stations along the A55. We struck lucky when ANPR picked up her car entering and leaving in a close time frame."

"How much in total?"

"Seven and a half grand."

"Not that much when you consider she dropped nineteen on a piece of tat." Macpherson nodded to the other information Cook had retrieved and printed in her search, including a printout of the white gold chain and pendant Reilly had discovered.

"So, where are we here? She's spending heavily on a company credit card, one that she wouldn't officially be entitled to use, and if her husband is paying it off through company accounts that makes it one for HMRC rather than us," said Taylor.

"Even if it's bleeding the business to the point of ruin?" said Macpherson.

"Bigger spends than that, Doc," said Cook, dragging up another set of financial documents and a list of trades.

"Mahood explained to you that Quinn was involved in R&D to enhance the capability of their PV products. Over the last year, he has made monthly deposits to three companies, each over the past few months has folded. The money out forms the basis of the crisis in Helios; look at the numbers."

Taylor did, and they were staggering. What was more incredible was how Quinn had managed to keep the extent of the outgoings secret from Mahood.

"Mahood had a report and told Quinn to cease and desist," said Taylor.

"Well, he didn't, and he continued to accrue personal and business debt."

"He was running the company into the ground," said Taylor, Quinn's duplicity faintly evident in the plethora of numbers up on the screen.

"Why?"

Taylor shook her head, losing the thread she had just grasped, the complexities of the accounts blurring her vision.

"Why risk all he had worked for? Mahood's an arsehole but surely he wasn't going to this extreme to out him?" said Macpherson, he had also looked away from the screen and was doodling, tap-tapping his pen as he eased across some of the paperwork, more comfortable with the tactile nature of sifting hard physical evidence than digital forensic accounting.

"All the testimony we have says Quinn put that company over everything, what could change that?" Taylor let the worm burrow, the question rhetorical and neither Macpherson nor Cook interrupted her thoughts.

"Guv?" Erin Reilly entered 4.12, closely followed by a glowing Walker.

"How'd it go?" said Taylor, nodding in greeting.

"Positive ID on Raymie Kilburn."

Macpherson thudded a closed fist on the table, giving his younger colleagues an approving wink as Reilly continued.

"Di Pearson's reports are also coming in," she said.

Macpherson pushed aside the documents as he, Taylor and

Cook made room for their colleagues.

"Go ahead," said Taylor.

"Confirmation of blood on the log. Tests return it as O-Negative. Adrian Quinn is O negative. Also, a quantity of blood and fibres in the bag and on the clothes match those in the car identifying them as belonging to Adrian Quinn."

There was a release of breath around the table as the news sank in and wheels started spinning. Quinn's clothes had been dumped a few hundred metres from his vehicle, and it was now looking like he was never coming back from his run. So much for worrying about how much of his company was going to be left or why he had been burning the proverbial house down.

"Soil samples on the trainers confirm flora and soil type correspond to the path but not to the deposition site…" Reilly paused as she scanned the next line on the report. "The log also carried skin sample traces which are being run through DNA, however, the bin bag containing the clothing held further fibres and fingerprint matches to a nominal already held on the database." Reilly looked up. "Raymond Kilburn."

"Chris, advise Sergeant Harris to have his sections be on the lookout for Kilburn and when you get the nod, I want him in here. Carrie, I need more CCTV footage from in and around the estate and the park. It's going to be crucial in proving he returned after that initial fracas with Quinn."

Chapter 20

The team had moved from 4.12 to the section briefing room, which was small and now overcrowded with the addition of Sergeant Harris and two crews from section four. Cook had remained behind and was trawling the Drumkeen Estate CCTV and ANPR cameras along the A55 in an attempt to confirm Kilburn's movements and spot his return to the forest park.

The uniforms of Section Four stood at the back of the room facing Taylor, who had taken a seat on the edge of a table positioned at the front where, to her right, Erin Reilly tacked up a picture of Raymond Kilburn and neatly printed his details on a whiteboard.

"Raymond Kilburn, Flat 3C Drumkeen Walk. Evidence is building up that Kilburn may have knowledge or be behind the disappearance of Adrian Quinn and should now be considered a suspect." Taylor took the time to look each of the uniforms in the eye as she continued the brief. Macpherson had adopted an at ease posture, hands behind his back and rocking back and forth on the balls of his feet, the motion and the crunching of the last of his brandy balls bleeding off his impatience.

Reilly moved to her inspector's left beside Walker; both were wearing body armour and had fastened utility belts with holstered Glock sidearms, extendable batons and TETRA radios around their waists. Walker fiddled with his earpiece, trying to get the balance of comfort and snug fit.

"Sergeant Harris has been notified by Mike-Eight that the suspect is at home so the plan is to head over there and affect the arrest of Raymond Kilburn, returning him here to Musgrave Street for questioning." She turned to indicate her two junior colleagues.

"The arresting officers are going to be DCs Reilly and Walker. Any questions?"

Taylor waited a beat but no one raised any concerns and each nodded, eager to get the show on the road.

"Okay, you're all clear. Get your PPE on, and any issues or escalation at the scene, report asap. Section Four, two of you with DC Reilly and Walker at the front, two of you round the back. I don't want a runner. Everyone else, usual cordon positions. Good luck."

❖❖❖

Taylor pulled out her chair and sat. Behind her, Macpherson closed the door to the interview room and a moment later the magnetic lock engaged with a dull click; he took the seat to his inspector's right.

The arrest of Raymond Kilburn had gone smoothly. Reilly and Walker had presented at the door and he had come without a fuss. The suspect now sat in an open-necked black shirt and dark jeans, his expression under the maturing black eye and bruises slipped between amusement and curiosity.

The solicitor, sitting to his left, was the more on edge of the two men and it seemed to Taylor his call for service had interrupted a set at the tennis club. She had seen him before but couldn't recall the name. He was mid-thirties and smelled of shower gel. His dark hair was still damp and there was a redness to his face and a disorder to the paperwork he shuffled that suggested more haste and less speed was required. Hoskins or Hopkins, she thought, definitely no closer to a Christian name as she checked her notes. His name was entered in the attendance checkbox, Jeremy Hoskins. Hoskins shrugged off his casual jacket and a crescent of perspiration peeked from under the armpits of his light blue polo shirt. A self-conscious sixth sense made him look up and he offered a quiet nod of acknowledgement that he was ready.

Taylor gave Kilburn a few more seconds under her stare before she pressed the discreet button on the edge of the desk.

Along the hall, in the observation room, Carrie Cook and an officer from the custody team were gathered around the mixing equipment and the digital video and voice recorders monitoring interview room four. Reilly and Walker had returned to Drumkeen Walk to follow up on any forensic opportunities that may present inside Kilburn's residence and Taylor had just taken a follow-up call from Reilly prior to entering the interview.

The recording system's dual tone broke the silence, a flat tone followed by a higher pitch.

"Interview commences at four thirty-eight pm. Present in the room, Detective Inspector Veronica Taylor, DS Macpherson. Mr Hoskins, representing the suspect, and…"

"Raymond Kilburn."

"You know why you're here, Raymond?"

"Yous think I offed that Quinn fella." Kilburn's face was impassive, his demeanour calm. The experience was not a new one for him.

"I believe you may know more about the disappearance of Adrian Quinn than the account you gave my officers yesterday," said Taylor.

"You can believe all you want, I don't know where he is."

"Pull the other one, Raymie, it plays the sash." Macpherson leaned forward, his expression saying he wasn't buying a word of it.

"Sure it was old, and it was beautiful." Kilburn sang the first of the lyrics to the popular loyalist ballad at Macpherson and then broke into a laugh, his eyes turning to linger on Taylor.

"Have you any evidence to corroborate your theory, Inspector?" said Hoskins, cutting over Kilburn's chuckles, everything about his manner saying he wanted the interview over with. Taylor gave the solicitor a nod and he scratched out a note he had made in a supermarket brand A4 spiral pad.

"We have an eyewitness who places you in Drumkeen Forest Park yesterday morning. They suggest you and Mr Quinn had a disagreement."

"I reported him for that," said Kilburn with a grin.

The monitor on the wall flickered, the rifle green background and PSNI logo replaced by a window showing a still image of the busy A55 dual carriageway.

"This is an ANPR image taken yesterday at seven thirty-seven am. Do you recognise the car?"

"Which one?"

"Raymie, we're not having a laugh here. A man's missing, a family man. He's three wee kids at home wondering why he hasn't come home to them."

If she thought appealing to his better nature would work, she was wrong. Kilburn pulled a face.

"The car in the centre of the image is a blue Ford Everest. Registered to you." Taylor paused and Cook duplicated the image on her monitor, the screen now showing grainy footage from the entrance to Drumkeen Forest. Kilburn's vehicle caught as it rattled over a cattle grid.

"Seven thirty-nine am, you enter the car park which corroborates the eyewitness statement."

"So what, I was there same time as him. So were twenty

other people."

"Nobody else had followed him up the road, boxed his car in and then chased him into the woods," said Macpherson.

"I didn't chase him."

"No?"

"No."

"What's your version?" said Taylor.

"I told the other two, he nearly ran me and my dog down, I wanted a word."

"Raymie, we've the benefit of having your record here. You're not the type to leave it with just a word."

"Mr Kilburn's previous convictions have no bearing on this case," said Hoskins.

"They give a quare account of his character though, don't they, Raymie?" said Macpherson with a wink

"No comment."

"When was this alleged hit and run?"

"I'm not exactly sure."

"You're not sure. Okay, so tell us about your injuries?"

Kilburn pointed to his face. "What's to tell."

"Quinn assaulted you?"

"I cornered him and put him straight on his driving and he lifted a log and hit me a thump."

"Image Bravo, seven, one, A."

In the observation suite, Cook dragged up the corresponding images taken at the scene and then at the forensic laboratory in Seapark.

"Is that it?" said Taylor. Kilburn shrugged.

"If you say so."

"You've two cracking shiners, big fella, but not much in the way of cuts," said Macpherson. Kilburn didn't answer and Hoskins had sat back in his seat, arms folded and looking weary.

"What DS Macpherson is telling you, Raymie, is that there

was blood detected on the log. That blood belongs to the same blood group as Adrian Quinn."

She waited as Cook introduced the close-ups of the bloodied stump onto the screen, all eyes watching the images scroll from the branch in situ on the grass to a white and brightly illuminated bench in the lab, the item then framed with forensic measurement tape and notations.

"Do you want to tell me how it got there?"

Kilburn shifted in his seat, his expression darkening. Taylor could see him replay events in his head.

"Losing your touch, Raymie. You didn't see it coming, did you?" Macpherson laughed. "I'd have paid to be there to see your face when he whacked you."

"Aye, he thought he was the big lad…" Kilburn rocked his two closed fists together.

"You taught him otherwise?"

Hoskins sat forward to speak, but Kilburn got in first.

"Did you think I was going to let him get away with it? With doing this to me?"

Kilburn again pointed at his face, his cheeks aglow, and his breathing heavy as the wash of his anger and aggression crashed over the table.

"What happened then?" said Taylor

"Once you started you couldn't stop?" added Macpherson.

Kilburn scoffed.

"You don't know what you're talking about."

"DC Cook?" said Taylor.

The image changed to the forest glade and a bag of discarded clothing, a close-up of a bloodstain, and a carefully snipped section of black plastic bin liner.

"These items were recovered from nearby where we believe an assault on Adrian Quinn took place. The items are identified as belonging to him."

"Never seen them before."

"There are multiple fibres which are currently being forensically processed. We'll run them against matches of clothing we have recovered from your flat that match those the eye witness described."

"Go ahead."

"Image Bravo, nine, two, C shows a section of bin liner that contained the clothing. Can you explain why your fingerprints are on the bag?"

Hoskins suddenly looked wide awake. Kilburn let out a loud, bellowing laugh.

"Piss off."

"You're in the system, big lad, the evidence doesn't lie," said Macpherson.

"Is this a fucking fit-up?"

Taylor shook her head. Hoskins was scribbling more notes. She caught his eye and played her ace.

"Raymie, following your arrest, officers searched your home and found a large sum of cash. Can you explain where you got it?"

"No comment."

Taylor had printed the images she received from Reilly from the flat in Drumkeen Walk. She drew them from a document folder she had on the table. First was the cash bundled in a black bin liner similar to that in which the clothes were deposited, and the next image was one of the notes laid out on what must have been Kilburn's dining table.

"That's twelve grand of cash. I need an explanation."

"No comment."

"Did you rob Adrian Quinn of that money?" said Taylor.

"What?"

"We know Mr Quinn had access to large quantities of cash, did you rob Adrian Quinn and in the process hurt or injure him so that he was left incapacitated?"

"No…"

"Inspector, might I confer with…" Hoskins blurted.

"Adrian Quinn was in debt. Had he approached you for a loan? Was he unable to pay back what he owed and as a result you hurt or injured him so that he was left incapacitated?"

"I fucking don't know where he is!"

"Did you kill Adrian Quinn and afterwards make attempts to hide his clothing and similarly his body in Drumkeen Forest Park?"

"I only gave him the bloody slap he deserved for doing this to me!" shouted Kilburn.

"We have a witness who places you at the scene. Your prints on a bag of his clothes. Give us a few more days and we will find DNA and fibres relating to you on those articles, and the cash we will match to withdrawals Adrian Quinn was making from ATMs at nearby service stations each morning."

"It's not his bloody money." Kilburn had both fists on the table, his voice rising, drowning out Hoskins' protests for a break.

"Raymond Kilburn, up until this point you have been arrested on the suspicion of…"

"They're fitting me up! I didn't take his money…"

"You are now officially accused of…"

"She gave me the money to keep my trap shut!" bellowed Kilburn.

Taylor stopped speaking. Macpherson's eyes narrowed to slits.

"Who gave you the money?" said Taylor into the silence.

"His missus. Quinn's wife."

"What for?"

"So I wouldn't tell him that she was knocking off his bloody mate behind his back."

Chapter 21

Aoife Quinn flinched. The harsh metallic buzz that announced the unlocking of the security gate was enough to set the teeth on edge, let alone when it combined with the rasp of hinges in need of a good oil.

As Macpherson pushed the screaming gate aside, Taylor led Quinn into the custody corridor, her hand firmly on the forearm of the nervous woman. The lift had been straightforward and without incident. Taylor and Macpherson were waiting when the woman returned to Bladon Manor after the school run, her queries turning to incredulity and then quiet compliance when asked to accompany them to Musgrave Street.

Following Kilburn's revelation, Taylor had called time on his interview and had him placed in the cells pending further questioning, granting Jeremy Hoskins the reprieve he had been yearning for, and her team time to dig into the allegations.

As she guided Quinn along the corridor the echo of a dull sonorous bang sounded, just another background noise the two officers automatically filtered out but one which gave Quinn a start. The unmistakable metallic thud of a cell door slamming closed was hopefully enough to reinforce the mental image Taylor wanted in the forefront of Aoife Quinn's mind as she put her in the interview seat.

Along the corridor to the right, Raymie Kilburn resided behind one such heavy door. They had enough to hold him, and given the evidence Taylor expected Seapark to follow through with, it was likely by the end of the day she would have enough to charge. What she now needed to ascertain though was if he had acted alone and in retaliation to Adrian Quinn's objectionable driving or was there something more sinister afoot.

Up ahead, their images were captured on a trio of wall-mounted monitors hanging on metal arms above the custody sergeant's booking-in desk. Taylor felt Quinn stiffen as she caught sight of herself in the display and coming under the impassive gaze of the custody sergeant. He stood patiently, hands flat on the countertop, the panelling that boxed in his domain festooned with contact details for duty representation, department head phone numbers, warnings of CCTV in operation and the reminders of the official bureaucracy that needed to be followed by all who entered his domain.

As they approached the booth, another corridor fed from the right, ending in a similar metal gate to the one they had just entered.

"Aoife Quinn, attending for a voluntary interview," said Taylor. The sergeant nodded, reaching for a thick black book.

"Sign in, please." He pushed the open book across to Quinn. A black biro was attached to the cover with a measure of string and a wad of Sellotape.

"Are you carrying any of the following?" He pointed at a laminated card mounted to his left showing a selection of contraband items, and then a small white plastic basket. "If so, may I ask that you deposit them here until you're signing out."

Quinn took a glance, then shook her head, reaching out a

trembling hand to take the pen, her scribble and attention distracted by the harsh buzz of the second access gate. Taylor suppressed a smile as Macpherson plucked the pen out of Quinn's hand and slid the book back to the custody sergeant.

Thirty metres away, Erin Reilly entered first. Behind her, Jackie Mahood reluctantly followed with Chris Walker's hand on his shoulder.

"Thanks, Mrs Quinn," said Taylor, loud enough to project to the ears of the approaching Helios director. "If you just come this way, we'll take your statement."

Quinn forced her gaze away from the approaching Mahood, his expression darkening at the sight of her.

As Macpherson held the door open, Taylor guided Quinn through and on towards the interview suite.

So far, so awkward. Mission accomplished.

Chapter 22

"Do you recognise this man?"

Having already fulfilled her obligations to the recording and ensuring Quinn was settled with a beaker of water and confirming her understanding she was there voluntarily and consenting to questions regarding her husband's disappearance, Taylor presented an eight by ten copy of Raymond Kilburn's mugshot taken a little under twelve hours before.

Aoife Quinn cut a forlorn figure. She had adopted a similar position to that from the sofa in her home, albeit made more uncomfortable by the hard, narrow chair on which she now sat, her eyes down and hands clamped between her thighs, Taylor suspected the former was to hide the shock of her recent sighting of Mahood, and the latter to better hide the nervous tension as she stared at the picture on the table.

"Mrs Quinn?"

Quinn glanced up, then back down, but made no answer.

"Mr Kilburn is in custody. We have reason to believe he was the last person to see your husband. When we spoke to you yesterday, we informed you of the recovery of clothes matching the description of your husband's. I can confirm after forensic analysis they are his," said Taylor.

Aoife Quinn sat stock still, the shallow rise of her breast

and the slight flare of her nostrils the only movement.

"Do you know this man, Aoife?"

Quinn gave an almost imperceptible nod.

"You're nodding, that's good. Can you tell us how you know him?" said Taylor.

"What about Adrian? Have you found him?" Quinn's voice was small. Taylor shook her head.

"No. We still don't know Adrian's whereabouts. I need to be clear here, Aoife. We found blood on Adrian's clothes and an eyewitness places this man with your husband on the morning of the disappearance so it's imperative you tell us how you know him."

"I..." Quinn's eyes dropped to her lap. Macpherson nodded to Taylor, indicating the document wallet in front of her. The inspector drew out the list of Helios expense transactions.

"We followed up on the twins' hospital appointment. It checked out." Taylor laid a finger on a line item that had been highlighted blue. Quinn followed the finger and then looked into Taylor's eyes as she continued.

"However we are able to say, based on CCTV evidence and the balance of probability, these other fifteen transactions were carried out by you."

Quinn remained silent, her eyes falling unfocused on the damning document.

"We know your husband was in financial difficulty. Did he approach this man for a loan?" said Macpherson, attempting to break the spell.

"Aoife, what were the ATM withdrawals for? Was Adrian paying this man off, or were you?" said Taylor.

A single tear fell from the corner of Quinn's left eye. Taylor pulled Reilly's photo of the cash from Kilburn's flat.

"This a significant sum of cash recovered at Raymond Kilburn's flat. It matches the sum withdrawn, by you, across various ATMs over the past few weeks." Macpherson spoke gently, trying to tease a reply.

"Aoife, help us understand why? It won't take much for us to match this cash to the batch that was issued from the ATM. You do understand how this looks?"

Quinn blinked away more tears. Taylor pulled a packet of tissues from her pocket and passed them across. Quinn took one and dabbed her eyes, taking a ragged breath and shaking her head.

"He approached me."

"This man?" said Taylor, eager to hear it.

"Yes."

"When?"

"Eight, ten weeks ago?"

"Where?"

Quinn shook her head and snorted in derision.

"At the kids' school. I was waiting in the car."

"And what did he say?"

"He told me he knew Jackie." Quinn's voice cracked as she spoke his name. She covered up the discomfort with a blow of her nose.

"And he told you he knew about the affair?" said Taylor, watching Quinn keenly as the words sank in. For a long moment, she said nothing and then her chin dropped, and she uttered a quiet hiss of affirmation.

"Kilburn says this cash came from you. Can we establish right now that is true?"

Quinn nodded, dabbing more tears.

"Was he blackmailing you?"

"He said he would tell Adrian," she said with a nod. "It was a stupid, stupid mistake."

"Did you tell Jackie?"

Quinn was still shaking her head in bitter regret as she answered. "He said he would sort it."

"How?"

Quinn shook her head, a memory etched on her face.

"Did he offer him money?"

"Jackie wouldn't spend on Christmas, and he certainly wouldn't be blackmailed."

"Are you saying he threatened your man?" said Macpherson, making a note to the list of follow-ups they would need to ask Kilburn.

"Whatever he did, it didn't work. He came to me again, and I told him I'd pay him to shut up."

"Aoife, are you and Jackie Mahood still having a relationship?" said Taylor. Quinn's face cracked, and the tears began to flow with abandon.

"It just happened… I was angry… angry about Katherine… angry about Aido putting the business first, again…"

"Aoife, do you know where Adrian is? Do you know if anything has happened to him?" Taylor leaned forward, her words landing with sobering clarity on the woman opposite.

"No…" The denial was abrupt, her face surprised. Taylor slid out an image of her husband's running gear. The one shoe and a snapshot of blood.

"You knew Adrian's route, his routine," she said.

"What? Why is that…"

"Did you conspire with Raymond Kilburn to kill your husband to conceal your affair and claim life insurance to secure the debts Adrian had accrued against your family home?"

Quinn looked horrified. She swallowed, her face blanching a peculiar shade of pale green and Taylor thought she might be about to vomit.

"No…"

"Did Jackie Mahood?"

Chapter 23

Taylor sipped a coffee, and Macpherson sucked the remnants of an iced finger from his thumb and forefinger. They had withdrawn from Aoife's interview and returned to the adjoining observation suite to join Carrie Cook.

She had drawn up two screens on the large observation monitor which they now watched; one showing Aoife Quinn and the other, Jackie Mahood. While the former had an expression wracked with tension and looked fragile, worn out and on the fringe of breakdown, Mahood, by contrast, was as bullish as ever. His demeanour was contemptuous, arms folded high on his chest, legs akimbo and leaning back in his seat, the front two legs beating a rhythm as he rocked back and forth.

"Not as naïve as Mrs Quinn," observed Cook. Macpherson snorted, taking a slurp of tea and shaking his head impatiently, Mahood having stalled the process in his request for having his solicitor present.

"No sign of the brief yet?" said Taylor, looking at her watch. Cook responded with a shake of the head.

"Should we pull Kilburn out again?" said Macpherson.

"Wait until we've had a crack at him," said Taylor, aiming her cup at the screen. Mahood stared back as though he were the one watching them.

A series of short beeps emitted from the observation suite code lock and the door opened. Reilly entered first, followed by a smiling Chris Walker.

"Great timing, Guv," he said, beaming from ear to ear. "Couldn't shut the bugger up until he saw you and heard Quinn was about to spill."

Taylor returned his enthusiastic smile and Macpherson slapped his younger colleague on the back as he sat down.

"Just what we wanted, son. Well done, the pair of you."

"How did you get on?" said Reilly. Taylor pursed her lips.

"She's admitted to the affair and for paying off Kilburn. One of which isn't a crime, and the other makes her the victim."

"What about smiler?" said Macpherson, nodding to the screen.

"Mr Personality?" said Reilly. "You weren't wrong. He went off on one and the first person he pointed the finger at was…." Reilly pointed her index finger at the screen showing Aoife Quinn.

"And they say chivalry is dead," said Cook.

"What did he say?" said Taylor.

"What you'd expect. He doesn't know where Quinn is and if anyone does, it's his missus. Then we took a healthy dose of slabbering about how to conduct our investigation and how he gave us evidence they were thieving from the business and nothing has been done."

"You kept a lid on Kilburn and the affair."

Reilly and Walker nodded in unison.

"Good," said Taylor. "I want to go through what we have again. All actions, those we covered and anything either just in or that remains outstanding."

She jettisoned her empty cup into an overflowing wastepaper basket and sat to Cook's right. Her train of thought had coalesced over the last twenty-four hours to form the opinion something untoward had happened to Adrian Quinn.

It wasn't a huge leap of deduction considering they had his clothes and evidence of his altercation with Kilburn, but the reasoning behind it was now more complex and troubling. All the information and verbal testimony had initially pointed to a meticulous and intelligent individual with the world at his feet, but what had caused the deterioration in his attitude towards his business partner, the excessive risks he had taken to drive that business forward and the compilation of massive debts threatening his home sat just outside her grasp.

Had the wool been pulled by Mahood and Quinn; were they behind the company's dwindling fortunes? Aoife Quinn certainly had been bashing the plastic, and Mahood by his own admission had put a noose on Adrian Quinn's spending, but it was he who had ultimately called time on the business. Had the adulterous couple tried to push Quinn out for their own gain, and if that hadn't worked or if he had found out would they have had the guts to make a final, brutal bid to ensure they stayed together and became wealthier as a result? Despite it looking like Helios was falling into administration, Chief Superintendent Law's simple query continued to burrow into her ear; where is the money?

"We need to link these three and we need to establish if Kilburn returned to the forest park. Any joy on CCTV first?"

"I've trawled the ANPR and CCTV available in and around the Drumkeen Estate," said Cook, her tone somewhat deflated. "Other than what we have of the morning, I've no images of Kilburn returning by vehicle, so the supposition is he returned on foot from his flat on Drumkeen Walk. We've nothing in the way of coverage if that's the case."

"Erin?"

"Laura Roberts gave a positive ID," said Reilly.

"And she's offered to supply the rest of the footage from the RSPB headquarters building. I've made arrangements to recover it," added Walker.

Macpherson chortled. "I'm sure you have. This doll must be something? You've been running about like a puppy with two tails since you first went over there. First, it's conservation and petitions, then you're dickied up like you fell out of Millets window…"

Walker blushed. "Millets doesn't…"

Macpherson waved the protest away.

"That's good, Chris," said Taylor. "We need something that places Kilburn back at the scene to establish him as being behind the dumping of Quinn's clothes so any CCTV of him on foot will be gold."

"What about any other eyewitnesses?" said Cook.

"None from the appeal," said Taylor.

"Laura didn't mention any further sightings?" said Macpherson with a pointed look at Walker.

"Nothing from her or the ground staff," confirmed Reilly, sparing Walker his blushes.

"We're going to struggle without a body," said Taylor.

"Search teams have scaled back but we're still combing the forest park. That being said, it's a huge area." Reilly shrugged.

Taylor thought for a moment.

"Did we ever get the GPS back on Quinn's motor?"

Cook nodded.

"Yes. It arrived at the park on the morning he went missing, the route matches ANPR and it didn't move until we had it towed." Cook's fingers darted across her keyboard and she pulled up a report and map showing the built-in GPS data attributed to Adrian Quinn's BMW. Attached to the report from technical services was a map of recent and regular locations, each pinpointed by geo coordinates.

Taylor nodded, the consideration that perhaps Quinn had been moved in his own car after the sighting now defunct.

"Okay, where are we on financials?"

Cook killed the GPS screen and launched a new window of transactions, one Taylor recognised and another she didn't.

"Jesus, I'll be seeing those numbers in my sleep," said Macpherson. "I'm away to get another round in. Same again?"

"I'll go," said Walker standing. He collected his mobile phone and shrugged at Macpherson. "Call of nature."

"Call of the naturist more like. You give her a call while you're out and rustle up the CCTV, oh, and see if you can get another one of those iced fingers while you're at it." Macpherson rubbed his eyes as Walker left the room and he returned his attention to the monitor. "Go on then, but remember maths isn't my strong suit."

Cook chuckled as she drew out the data, giving a nod to Reilly.

"We consolidated the information we got from the card and the complaint Mahood issued. A good proportion of that spend is ATM withdrawals, the transactions we can link to Aoife Quinn and her spend across the city."

"It was burning a hole in her pocket alright," said Macpherson. "Mahood wasn't going to need to be a forensic accountant to spot his money was being spent on shoes and jewellery."

"Up until now, we've assumed Quinn had issued her the card. What if it was Mahood? A perk for the mistress?" said Reilly.

Taylor nodded, considering the viewpoint. It was one way Quinn may have stumbled on his wife's indiscretions, and if he had and challenged them, it would be the simple answer to how a conflict developed.

"The transactions on that card all fall within a geographical boundary that runs along the A55 for ATM withdrawal and in and around the city centre for spend," said Cook, a map superimposed now on the screen and she used the cursor to point out the broader area and locations. "We have found another card linked to the Helios business account that has also been active during the same period and following the same pattern of activity as the first."

The desk phone rang. Taylor picked up the receiver, returning it a few moments later after a short conversation.

"Mahood's brief is delayed. He's finishing up in court now so it could be another hour," she said. Macpherson looked at his watch and groaned. That would mean any interview would be cutting into dinner time.

"Sorry, Carrie, crack on."

"The second card follows a similar pattern of ATM withdrawals although outside the other card's geographical boundary; in saying that, it does share one common retail hit. A high-end jewellery store. Callan's of Ann Street."

The name was familiar to Taylor and she could place the black shop front where it sat on the corner of the main pedestrian precinct, but not how it related to the case. Cook shifted the map view and again used the cursor to point out the broad scope of the card's travels. As the cursor cut east across the suburbs, she highlighted four locations they knew to be ATMs. A Sainsbury's store at a retail park off the main A2 carriageway, a filling station on the A20 close to the Ulster Hospital and several others at retail parks further outside the city. Taylor's train of thought caught, crashing to a stop as suddenly as a head-on collision.

"Carrie, go back," she said. Cook glanced at her sharply, the sudden impetus in the inspector's voice crystal clear.

"To the other card...?"

"No back, back. The tech services report on Quinn's GPS data."

The door to the observation suite opened, and Walker entered.

"For God's sake you're asked to do one job—" said Macpherson, his words tumbling to a halt as he caught the younger man's expression. Walker carried no cups and no iced finger. His complexion was as white as the wall.

Cook clicked back through the screens until she had the technical service report and the map of Quinn's locations.

Taylor spotted the pattern now she knew what to look for.

"Guv…" Walker's voice caught with a block of emotion, and Macpherson stood fearing he was about to fall. Walker held out his phone.

Taylor looked at the display and then back to the details Cook had put on screen. She gave a short nod, the single image embedding a hook in what seconds ago might have been conjecture. She handed the phone to Macpherson.

"Ack, Christ," he said with a sad shake of the head, glancing up before looking back down at the screen to confirm what he was seeing, a case of innocent Facebook stalking gone horribly wrong. He shook his head again. "You poor bugger."

Chapter 24

The clouds that obscured the low-lying sun painted a purple palette across the sky above Strangford Lough, while below, the cold waters of the inlet were rippled by strong currents and eddies that earned the beguiling and beautiful stretch of water its dangerous reputation.

Macpherson negotiated the narrow lane from the main Portaferry Road towards a stony car park that clung to a rocky cove on the water's edge, as the car crunched down the track. Both his own and Taylor's eyes were drawn beyond an old sea wall where, rising from the gloom of the waves and trailing a white plume of water, stood the world's first commercial tidal stream power station.

"I didn't even know this was here," said Macpherson, the Volvo taking a crunching dip as it entered the car park and he eased the car to a stop.

"I've a vague memory about it launching, but yeah, it's still a bit of a surprise to most I guess."

SeaGen loomed out of the water like the bulbous periscope from a Bond villain's lair or the conning tower of a futuristic submarine. The underwater tidal electricity generator took advantage of the fast tidal flow of the lough to drive its powerful turbines and in turn generate enough electricity to power thousands of the surrounding peninsula's homes.

"I said it once and I'll say it again, I'm some mentor." Macpherson ratcheted on the handbrake and gave Taylor an approving nod. She smiled sadly.

"It's easy when it's staring you in the face." She raised the image they had printed from Walker's phone.

Taylor pulled her jacket and scarf tighter as she exited the car. The wind that whipped off the sea inlet was cold and the waning sun would do little to oblige them with any heat from behind its impressionist canvas.

The dog's head snapped up sharply at the sound of Macpherson closing his door, the small terrier uttering a series of staccato barks at the strangers.

Macpherson fell into step beside Taylor as they approached, the small dog dancing in excited circles around the feet of its owner.

"Ms Roberts?"

Taylor raised a hand as they got closer. The dog's low rumbling was audible over the keening of the wind.

Laura Roberts squinted into the breeze, plucking a hair from her mouth as she stooped to secure the dog on its lead. As she stood back up, Taylor caught the gleam of white gold under her unzipped gilet. A long chain lay against the dark material of her sweater, on the end of which hung a distinctive pendant.

"I wondered how long it would take." Roberts shushed the growling dog and turned towards the low sea wall and the spectacle of the tidal generator. "I have to admit, when your colleagues called to the house I thought that was it."

Taylor fell into step to the woman's right, the terrier's little brown face staring up as it trotted along, a bit more calm but still straining against the lead. Its interest in the newcomers and what treats they had, if any, piqued.

"It took a bit of putting the pieces together but we usually get there in the end," said Taylor.

Roberts gave a small huff of laughter but there was a sadness in her eyes. She gave the dog a measure of leash as they approached the edge of the car park. The wall was broken by a set of pillars offering a way to a crescent of stony beach and the water's edge beyond, and as they neared, they saw a figure casting off, stood at the water's edge, another fishing rod sitting on a tripod to the left beside a dark tackle box.

As her feet hit the stony shale and crushed shell, Taylor watched the figure turn, a sudden shaft of light breaking from the edge of the clouds to frame him in a golden spotlight.

She stopped ten feet away. Macpherson—as always—was at her shoulder. The mystery solved but a hundred questions yet to be answered.

"Adrian Quinn?" she said.

Epilogue

Taylor watched from the end of the hallway as Reilly escorted Aoife Quinn from the custody sergeant's desk to the noisy gate that led to the car park and freedom. She turned at the sigh from behind.

"Is that it then?" said Walker.

Taylor nodded up at the monitor which showed Macpherson and Cook in deliberation with Kilburn and his solicitor. Mahood had already gone.

"Soon will be," she said.

Walker hung his head, and she felt a pang of sympathy for the young man but also a swell of contentment in knowing that a rough edge had been knocked off and he would, in time, reflect on a lesson learned. He wouldn't be the first and he wouldn't be the last to fall for the charms of a pretty young witness.

"Come on," she said, putting an arm around his shoulder and guiding him back up to 4.12.

Macpherson and Cook entered close behind them with Reilly coming in last but not least, the tray of tea and coffee and selection of pastries and cream buns raising Macpherson from his seat like he'd been stung.

"That's mine, thanks very much," he said, claiming the lone iced finger before there was any time for objections.

"Kilburn away?" said Taylor as he took a huge bite. Cook answered.

"Released without charge."

Taylor nodded, Kilburn's involvement, it seemed, had been a contrivance by the man to shake down Quinn for more cash by offering him information that he already knew. Kilburn's bash to the head and hours facing a potential murder charge seemed a fitting punishment for being greedy and playing two ends off against the middle, but in the end, Taylor reckoned it wouldn't be enough to have taught him a lesson.

The wall behind held the image of the technical services map and the list of financial transactions and other Helios trades uncovered by Cook over the last days.

"What did he have to say for himself?" said Cook, tearing apart a fresh cream apple turnover, Macpherson made to speak but his mouth was still full.

"He wasn't one bit sorry for the damage he's caused," said Taylor, declining the plate and instead, stirring her coffee. "Although to be fair he did have some guilt at giving us the runaround."

She thought back to the beach and the knowing look that crossed Adrian Quinn's face when he realised his few short days of peace and isolation were up. He had apologised immediately, but any remorse that he might have shown for the suffering he had caused his wife and his former business partner was conspicuously absent.

"He knew of the affair," she explained. "It had been ongoing for some time and reading between the lines it wasn't the first time Aoife had strayed. He alluded to the fact that her infidelities were what drove him to Katherine Clark, although he confirmed her story that it was a one-off. He's filing for divorce and joint custody of the kids."

All heads bowed at the thought of the upheaval and the impact on the three innocent lives.

"And Roberts?" said Reilly. She offered a sympathetic glance at Walker whose eyes remained fixed on the table. He hadn't taken a bite either, his pride damaged and the object of his crush suddenly plunged headlong into the arms of Adrian Quinn.

"Quinn and Roberts struck up a conversation at the forest park and one thing led to another. When the expansion deal was in full swing, Quinn found that Mahood had cut a deal without his knowledge to buy up the sites for the plant and the solar farms; he had Clark leak the news when Roberts informed him of an issue with one of the locations."

"The site acquired on the edge of Drumkeen Forest," said Walker. Taylor nodded. He had been doing his homework.

"The reason there were no building works on that site already was due to the nature of the substrate, it was sand based and a known area of flood risk because of its proximity to the River Lagan. Bad for development but five-star hospitality for migratory birds." Taylor took another sip of coffee. "Roberts had been trying to overturn the development order for years, designating the area as a protected wetland and pressing for specific status as it was a known breeding ground for the curlew."

All eyes now stared at the picture of the white gold chain and its pendant of the wading bird with the long curved beak. "According to Quinn, Mahood knew about him and Roberts and bought the land as a means to strong-arm him into handing over the majority share of Helios in exchange for release of the ground to the park trust."

"What Mahood didn't know was Quinn was a step ahead," said Macpherson sucking the icing off his fingers. Taylor continued.

"When Jackie Mahood bought into the business, Quinn had a non-compete drawn up. He knew Mahood had a habit of buying into firms, asset stripping and then setting up as a competitor but at the time he needed the finance. Quinn then found himself bound by the agreement, so he found a way around it."

Cook considered what they knew about Quinn's financials, his Helios trades both fair and foul and the state of the company as he had left it.

"He was stripping out the liquid assets…" she said

"To reinvest away from solar…" continued Reilly.

"And into tidal. He has secured a position with SeaGen to advance their tidal power capacity with the technical advances he made in Helios and offered to bring those advances and the key individuals essential to their integration across with him."

Macpherson shook his head. "You've got to hand it to him. Any wonder Mahood thought the money he was burning through was wasted. It wasn't meant for Helios in the first place."

"What will happen to him?" said Walker. "To Laura?"

Taylor smiled, the expression mirrored by her two female colleagues, as Macpherson rolled his eyes.

"Given the way Quinn went about things, he'll likely be struck off as a company director. Were his actions criminal? Probably not. Were they morally questionable? Definitely, although he believes all staff pensions are secure and any debts remain manageable through the administrators' sale of the remaining PV assets and his own intellectual properties. He was quite happy when he mentioned it wouldn't leave much for Mahood or his wife, though. As for Laura Roberts, other than her questionable taste in men, she answered the questions we asked and corroborates Quinn's side of the story. Yes, she ditched his bag of clothes but other than having the council issue her a fine for fly-tipping…."

"Lucky escape, son," said Macpherson, pushing back his chair and standing to ease out the cricks in his back. "Take it from me…"

"Brace yourselves for a lesson from the relationship guru," said Reilly, rising and stacking the cups.

"What are you talking about?" Macpherson scowled. "Twenty years I'm married. If I can find a woman to stick with me that long, I must have some tips to offer. Chris, come on and I'll tell you about the time…"

"Never mind him. Chris, give us a hand and we'll get these sorted and go for a drink. I'll buy," said Reilly.

Taylor shook her head in mirth as Macpherson's mouth dropped open.

"I'll buy," said Cook. "You can tell me about that petition. My dad was quite taken with it when I was telling him about the plight of Belfast's starlings."

"I'm not sure if I'm in the mood…"

"Right, fella." Macpherson pointed a finger and blustered. "There's two fine wee girls offering to buy you a drink and if you don't get up off your arse and take them up on it you're more of a buck eejit than I thought you were."

"Go on, the three of you," said Taylor. "We'll square up here and see you in the morning."

Reilly and Cook offered their thanks and Walker followed suit, rising with just a little reluctance, but seemingly brighter at the prospect of roping in Carrie, or at least her father, to his newfound passion.

"And I thought we only dispensed the good cop, bad cop routine on the villains?" said Taylor.

"You're too soft," said Macpherson, gathering some of the files and watching them go.

"I blame my mentor," said Taylor with a smirk. "Speaking of which, when are we going to discuss your transfer to the training college with the chief super?"

She ducked the flying files with a raucous laugh, the sound of it and Macpherson's swearing reaching far enough along the corridor to put a grin back on the face of a retreating Chris Walker.

Afterword

THANK-YOU FOR READING 'INTO THIN AIR'

I sincerely hope you enjoyed this Novella Case-File. If you can **please** spare a moment to leave a short review it will be very much appreciated and helps immensely in assisting others to find this, and my other books.

Follow Detective Inspector Veronica Taylor and her team in:

'BEHIND CLOSED DOORS' and 'CODE OF SILENCE'

You can find out about these books and more in the series by signing up at my website:

www.pwjordanauthor.com

Also by Phillip Jordan

ALSO BY PHILLIP JORDAN

THE BELFAST CRIME SERIES

CODE OF SILENCE
COMING SOON- THE CROSSED KEYS
COMING SOON- NO GOING BACK

THE BELFAST CRIME CASE-FILES

BEHIND CLOSED DOORS
INTO THIN AIR

THE TASK FORCE TRIDENT MISSION FILES

AGENT IN PLACE
COMING SOON- DOUBLE CROSS

Get Exclusive Material

GET EXCLUSIVE NEWS AND UPDATES FROM THE AUTHOR

Building a relationship with my readers is *the* best thing about writing.

Visit and join up for information on new books and deals and to find out more about my life growing up on the same streets that Detective Inspector Taylor treads, you will receive the exclusive e-book 'IN/FAMOUS' containing an in-depth interview and a selection of True Crime stories about the flawed but fabulous city that inspired me to write.

You can get this **for free,** by signing up at my website.

Visit at www.pwjordanauthor.com

About Phillip Jordan

ABOUT PHILLIP JORDAN

Phillip Jordan was born in Belfast, Northern Ireland and grew up in the city that holds the dubious double honour of being home to Europe's Most Bombed Hotel and scene of its largest ever bank robbery.

He had a successful career in the Security Industry for twenty years before transitioning into the Telecommunications Sector.

Aside from writing Phillip has competed in Olympic and Ironman Distance Triathlon events both Nationally and Internationally including a European Age-Group Championship and the World Police and Fire Games.

Taking the opportunity afforded by recent world events to write full-time Phillip wrote his Debut Crime Thriller, CODE OF SILENCE, finding inspiration in the dark and tragic history of Northern Ireland but also in the black humour, relentless tenacity and Craic of the people who call the fabulous but flawed City of his birth home.

Phillip now lives on the County Down coast and is currently writing two novel series.
For more information:

www.pwjordanauthor.com
www.facebook.com/phillipjordanauthor/

Copyright

* * *

FIVE FOUR PUBLISHING

Printed in Great Britain
by Amazon